THE BOTTLE IMP of BRIGHT HOUSE

by
TOM LLEWELLYN

illustrated by
GRIS GRIMLY

HOLIDAY HOUSE · NEW YORK

Library of Congress Cataloging-in-Publication Data
Names: Llewellyn, Tom (Thomas Richard), 1964-, author.
Title: The bottle imp of Bright House / Tom Llewellyn.
Description: First edition. I New York : Holiday House,
2018 I Summary: Thirteen-year-old Gabe buys a bottle bearing an imp
that will grant his every wish, but someone else will pay the price and,
if he dies while owning the bottle, he will lose his soul.
Identifiers: LCCN 2017024824 I ISBN 9780823439690 (hardcover)
Subjects: I CYAC: Wishes—Fiction. I Demonology—Fiction. I Apartment
houses—Fiction. I Family life—Washington (State)—Tacoma—Fiction.
I Tacoma (Wash.)—Fiction.
Classification: LCC PZ7.L7724 Bot 2018 I DDC [Fic]—dc23
LC record available at https://lccn.loc.gov/2017024824

To my family: Deb, Ben, Abel, Bizayehu,
and Genet. To all the wishes granted and all
the ones left hanging, to all the mysteries we
solved and all the ones beyond our fingertips,
to all the friends we welcomed at our kitchen
table and all the strangers we turned into
friends, to all the jokes, all the tears,
all the fires we survived, and to home.
Most of all, to home.

TABLE OF CONTENTS

YOUR LAST CHANCE TO ESCAPE

THIS STORY IS 98 PERCENT TRUE.

What I mean by that, Dear Reader, is that it's just as true as I can stand to make it.

Mrs. Appleyard said everyone lies. She knew better than most. Our late landlady lied all the time. And cheated. And ripped off everybody who lived in her building, the Bright House Apartments.

And by *late*, I don't mean she wasn't on time. *Late*, in this case, means *dead*. As in *the late Mrs. Appleyard*. Because I'm sure she's dead. Well, pretty sure.

When she was still alive, and when something would break in our apartment, Mom or Dad would send me across the street to tell Mrs. Appleyard. Across the street was a tavern called Hank's Bar. Mrs. Appleyard spent half her time in one of Hank's booths, staining the ceiling above her with against-the-rules cigarette smoke. I hated going over there, because I could never escape without a five-minute conversation. It would usually go something like this:

"Mrs. Appleyard, my mom wants me to tell you there's no water coming out of the shower."

"She does, does she? Then why doesn't she come over herself? Doesn't it seem strange to you that your mother—if she is your mother—sends a child to a tavern?"

"Yeah, well, the shower stopped working and she's got a head full of shampoo and no clothes on."

"What's her name, again? This woman you call your mother?" Mrs. Appleyard took a swallow from her glass of red, fizzy liquid.

"Umm—Kathleen."

"Kathleen. So she's Irish. And she doesn't want to come to the bar? But your last name is Silver. Isn't that Jewish?"

"I think English and some other stuff. I don't really know."

"You don't know? But you do know this Irish woman is your mother?"

"Yes, and I'm supposed to tell you—"

"The shower. I know. How do you know she's your real mother?"

"I'm pretty sure."

"Mr. Appleyard thought he knew his real parents, too. He eventually found out he was no relation. They bought him off a boat, if you can believe it, down at the docks. His parents took him home in a Styrofoam cooler, same way you'd take home a catch of Dungeness crab. Then they lied to him about it." She took another swallow of her red fizzy liquid. "It's been my experience, and continues to be my experience, that all people are liars. I know I'm one. In fact,

I'm going to lie right now." She smiled. "Tell your supposed mother I'll be right over."

That's a tiny sample—a little sip—of Mrs. Appleyard. I wished I could have found a way to avoid hearing her stories. But I didn't have a choice. My parents made me their message boy.

But you, Dear Reader, you have a choice. You can set this book down right now and go read a car magazine instead. You can go outside and run a race down the block against your best friend. You probably won't believe me, anyway. But this story is true. At least one little devil appears. At least one bone breaks. At least one person dies— maybe more. And the hot tub that comes out of nowhere— well, I'm just saying that it all happened. This is as close to the facts as I can stand to get.

Maybe you shouldn't believe. Maybe you'll sleep better if you don't. And maybe you should remember what Mrs. Appleyard said, about all people being liars.

I INTRODUCE YOU TO THE TENANTS, THE FRIEND, AND THE SOON-TO-BE-DEAD MAN

MY NAME IS GABE. But that's enough about me. And you've already met Mrs. Appleyard.

Next is a girl named Joanna. She causes all sorts of problems. She's in seventh grade, like me. I have permanent bruises on both arms because of her.

Henry's my best friend. Some people think we're related, like brothers or cousins, because they hardly ever see one of us without the other. I guess I could hang out with other people, but—I don't know—the truth is I'd rather just hang out with Henry, even if he drives me crazy sometimes. By the way, he used to be the catcher on our baseball team, before he broke his arm, but that comes later.

Mr. Shoreby is a really rich guy. Don't get too attached to him. He'll be dead soon.

Then there's Doctor Mandrake, who lives on the top floor of my building. He's the one who's gonna tell me not to lose my soul.

Turns out it's harder than it sounds.

Most of this story happened at the Bright House Apartments. The Bright House sat across the street from Hank's Bar, in Tacoma, Washington. Next to the bar was the Corner Store, where Mr. Kim sold beef jerky, expired candy, and car magazines wrapped in plastic. Don't worry about Mr. Kim. He doesn't come into play. In fact, let's not mention him at all after this. Let's get to what actually happens. The details.

Just remember, Dear Reader, the Devil is in the details.

Dad claimed the Bright House was white. That's what he said when he first gave Mom directions, before we moved in. "It's the big white building, right across from the store," said Dad. His voice was coming out of the speaker on Mom's phone.

"Across from the bar, you mean?" asked Mom. My little sisters and I were staring out the window of Mom's pool-cleaning van. "There is no white building. There's a brick building, but the sign on that says Gregor Manor. And next to that is an old gray thing."

"That's the one."

"Oh, Johann. You've got to be kidding me. You want us to live there?"

"I already signed the lease."

"You signed it? For how long?"

"One year."

"Johann, you can't be serious. The building looks like it's about to fall apart."

The Bright House Apartments building was shaped like a cube. I say *was*, Dear Reader, because it's not there anymore. When it was still standing, it was three stories tall

and had eight units. Actually, more like seven and one-quarter. On the first floor was Mrs. Hashimoto, a painter—she painted art, not houses. The floor outside her door was speckled with bits of red, blue, and black paint. I would not meet her for another two weeks.

Right next to her lived a man named Jimmy Hyde, who I soon learned seemed to do nothing except sit behind his locked door and play Hawaiian music. Which was fine by me. On the rare occasions when he did come out, he looked about a hundred years old, with a few wisps of white hair on his head, a face full of wrinkles, and a few brown teeth in his mouth.

Mrs. Appleyard lived in one big unit that took up one

whole side of the first floor. I don't know why she needed all that space, since she spent nearly all her time in Hank's Bar.

The quarter unit belonged to Alejandro Aguilar, the fix-it man. His tiny apartment was jammed under the stairs on the first floor.

"Alley Handro can help you with your heavy stuff," said Mrs. Appleyard on the first of May, the day we moved in. *Alley Handro.* That's how she said his name, all hard letters. Mrs. Appleyard had a glass of that red fizzy stuff in her hand. She drank it through a straw.

"He can help?" said Dad. "That would be great. See what a nice place this is, honey? They even help you move in."

Mom hefted a box without a word.

Our unit was on the second floor, along with two other families. In the small apartment next door lived "the weird girl with the sick mom," in the words of my sisters. Right across the hall from us was a family named Brackley. They were gone the day we moved in. "On some fancy vacation," said Mrs. Appleyard. "Fanciest folks in the building."

"See, honey?" said Dad, as he and Alejandro tried to angle our old, worn couch through our front door. "We're right across the hall from the best folks in the building."

Mrs. Appleyard sucked on her straw. "I didn't say the best. I said the fanciest."

"How many people live upstairs?" said Mom, glaring at the glass in the landlady's hand.

"Just the one," said Mrs. Appleyard. "Doc Mandrake."

"A doctor?" said Dad. "Honey, we've got a doctor living upstairs from us."

"He ain't a real doctor," said Mrs. Appleyard. "Can't help you with as much as an infected toenail. He's some sort of astro—what do you call it—he studies stars and planets and all that."

"An astronomer? A man of science?"

"Something like that."

"I'd rather have a real doctor," said Mom.

"You and me both," said Mrs. Appleyard, taking another suck on the straw. "Bunch of hocus-pocus if you ask me. Mr. Appleyard never did cotton to any of that moon-in-the-seventh-house-Age-of-Aquarius-hippy-dippy nonsense." She kept talking while Mom dropped her box in the hallway and went downstairs for another.

Alejandro and Dad muscled our old couch through our door and dropped it with a thud. Alejandro Aguilar was a white-haired man with light brown skin. When he finally finished jamming the last piece of furniture inside our apartment, he handed Dad a piece of yellow paper.

"What's this?" said Dad.

"This is a bill from Mrs. Appleyard."

"A bill? Two hundred dollars? But I already paid the rent."

"Not for rent," said Alejandro. "This bill is for moving fees."

Dad took the bill down to Mrs. Appleyard's apartment to complain, but she wasn't there. Alejandro pointed to the bar across the street. Dad marched the bill to Hank's. When he came back ten minutes later, I asked him what happened.

"Don't mention this to your mother," he said.

Our apartment was listed as a three-bedroom. That was a stretch. My parents had the biggest room, which was smaller than my bedroom in our old house. My sisters' bunk beds nearly filled their shared room. Their dresser touched the bed on one side and the wall on the other. Dad called it cozy. The only window in their room was cut in half by a wall.

My room was even skinnier, but longer. It was slightly less wide than a mattress, so we ditched my bedframe and just laid the mattress on the floor. Both sides curled up against the walls. The other half of the window from my sisters' room was at the end, just above my pillow.

"Johann, this isn't a bedroom. It's barely even a hall-way. Gabriel can't sleep here. His bed is like a trough."

"Cozy," said Dad. "Just think of it as cozy."

The living room and kitchen weren't too bad. No dining room. No entryway. But the weirdest features in the apartment were the white, circular fixtures on every wall. There were eight of them in the living room, eight in the kitchen, and four in each bedroom. Each one had a tiny red light that blinked every second.

"What are those things?" said Mom. "They look like smoke detectors."

"They *are* smoke detectors," said Dad. "Same kind as the one we had in our old house. I guess they really care about safety. That's good. Isn't that good, honey?"

"It's weird. It creeps me out."

Dear Reader, I would hear those smoke detectors go off one day. I would hear them all sing together, like some sort of screeching, electronic choir.

More smoke detectors lined the hallway, the stairs, and everywhere else throughout the building. When I said they creeped me out, too, Dad said, "Keep your thoughts to yourself, Gabe, because this place is all we can afford. Heck, we can't really even afford this, unless I get a better job somehow, somewhere."

"I don't see how you can't find a job," I said. "You've got so many degrees. I mean, *you're* a doctor, too."

"Doctors of sociology don't get jobs as easily as doctors of medicine," Dad said.

The university had fired Dad. Whenever I said that— that he was fired—Dad got all cranky. "I wasn't fired. They had to do some right-sizing. Someone had to go. It just happened to be me."

"Sounds like you *just happened* to get fired," I said.

Right now, Dad was teaching part-time at the community college during the day and delivering pizzas for Hasty's Pizza at night. His car smelled like pizza all the time.

Mom was a writer who didn't seem to make any money from the travel books she wrote. I wouldn't recommend buying one. I mean, she's never really done any traveling, except driving from pool to pool around Tacoma. She cleaned swimming pools and hot tubs while we were at school. Her van smelled like chlorine.

Both my parents' cars smelled like lousy jobs.

But Mom still wrote books about climbing Kilimanjaro, walking the Great Wall of China, and bicycling through Holland. As far as I knew, she'd never been to any of those places. If she'd gone, she sure hadn't taken me with her.

When Dad finished assembling our beds, he said he needed to go to work at Hasty's. "You're leaving now?" asked Mom. "We haven't even gotten the furniture situated."

"Gabriel can help you," said Dad. "He's practically a man now."

"Thirteen is not a man," said Mom.

Dad squeezed my arm, as if checking a peach to see if it was ripe. He shrugged, then left. For the next two hours, Mom ordered my sisters and me around until we got the living room in some kind of shape.

My sisters, Meg and Georgina, were nine-year-old twins. Georgina cut her own hair with scissors, "because the salon people never make it short enough." Georgina took after Mom. She wore hiking boots and helped Mom change the oil on both our cars. Meg was more interested in changing her nail polish, which she did precisely every three days.

When Mom finally let us go, I went into my bedroom to start decorating it.

Last night I'd slept in my room in our old house. It wasn't like the old house was anything special, but we'd had a backyard with a trampoline. Just the closet in my old room was almost as big as this whole room.

All day, Dad had kept telling me I should be grateful I had a roof over my head. I'd said, "It's not a roof. It's a floor. I have Doctor Mandrake's floor over my head."

I shoved my mattress up against the half window and put my dresser on the other end of the narrow room. There was no space next to my bed for my nightstand, so I put that at the foot end of my mattress.

I hung my car posters on the walls, starting at the far end with the orange McLaren F-1. Then came the 1961 blue Jaguar E-Type—the one that some people call the XK-E. After that was the yellow Lamborghini Miura. I'm not much of a Lamborghini fan, but Henry got me that poster for my last birthday, so I kind of had to hang it up. Then came the 1955 silver Mercedes-Benz 300SL, the 2004 Porsche Carrera GT, and the black AC Cobra with the two white stripes right up the middle.

The Cobra had been my favorite for years, because it was just so mean looking. That was until I saw the Ferrari 430. Four-thirty as in 430 horsepower. Top speed of 196 miles an hour.

Dear Reader, by now you probably get that I like cars. They go fast. They can take you anywhere. They look cool—at least the nice ones. Freedom, power, and coolness, just rolling down the road. So I like them. Maybe even love them. But I've never been in a position to do anything more than dream, because my mom and dad—like most grown-ups—seem to secretly hate cars. Or they hate the fact that they can't afford the good ones. Or maybe Mom and Dad hate cars because they're reminders that they don't have any freedom, don't have any power, and aren't cool.

The Ferrari 430 was the car in the poster closest to the head of my bed. Painted in Ferrari red, of course. Its body was so smooth and flowing it looked as much like a sea creature as it did a car. I would have given my right arm just to see one. I would have given both arms to own one.

Turned out, I'd get to keep my arms. I'd only have to give my soul.

A WARNING FROM DOCTOR MANDRAKE

I WOKE UP THE NEXT MORNING with the bright light from half a window shining on my face. I'd need to get a curtain for that if I planned on ever sleeping in. I wondered if you could buy curtains for half a window.

I walked into the living room and stepped into a puddle of water. I yelled for Mom and Dad. Dad stumbled out, stepped in the same puddle, then looked at the ceiling above, where a steady drip of water was falling.

Dad called Mrs. Appleyard. Half an hour later, she stood in our living room, staring up at the ceiling with another glass of red, fizzy liquid in her hand.

"A leaky pipe upstairs. I can fix it," said Mrs. Appleyard, wiping her mouth on the sleeve of her bathrobe. "But Alley Handro is pretty backed up on repairs right now. Prob'ly be a couple of weeks before he can get to it."

"A couple of weeks?" said Dad. "We're just supposed to live like this for a couple of weeks?"

"I can fix it sooner. Always can fix it sooner, Johann.

Two-hundred-dollar rush fee and you'll go straight to the top of the list."

"Why would I pay two hundred dollars? It's not even my apartment that's leaking."

"Not saying you *should* pay it. It's your choice."

Dad tapped his foot, splashing water. "The only reason we're living here is because we can't afford some place better. If you keep on charging us two hundred dollars every five minutes, then we're not saving any money."

"I ain't charging you, Johann," said Mrs. Appleyard. "I'm giving you *options*."

Dad wrote her a check and told me not to mention it to Mom.

"Top of the list," said Mrs. Appleyard, as she tucked the check inside the front of her robe. "Alley Handro'll be here in a jiff. You know, Mr. Appleyard would have liked this—it's like a little ocean right in the middle of your living space. Mr. Appleyard probably would have dropped a fishing line into it to see if he could catch anything. That man loved to fish. He once caught the world's second-biggest German brown trout in a kiddie pool at the county park. Only thing he loved more than fishing was arguing about politics. Fishing and politics. I never had interest in either one. They both make your breath stink." She talked about Mr. Appleyard until Dad herded her into the hallway and shut the door.

"Nice place, Dad." I said. "Real nice. I'm so happy I live here."

Dad glared at me. Mom came out of the bedroom, dressed for work.

"It's Sunday," said Dad. "What are you doing up so early?"

"Going to clean some pools," said Mom.

"On Sunday?"

"Took on three new customers this week."

"You're working too much," said Dad.

"Bills," said Mom. "Someone's got to pay them." She kissed Dad and left.

Mom and Dad had a decent relationship. By that I mean that they did a pretty good job of putting up with each other. Kind of like the way I put up with my friend Henry. Mom always said, "If you can't figure out how to put up with other people's shortcomings, then you're gonna live a lonely life."

Dad sopped up the water with a couple of pool towels, then put a bucket under the drip. When Meg got up and saw the half-filled bucket, she rushed back to her room and returned with a Barbie and a handful of tiny little bikinis. Georgina came with her own Barbie. Georgina had cut its hair short and was now coloring its naked body black with a Sharpie. I asked her what she was doing. "Putting on her wet suit. She's going diving."

I nodded out of respect for my sister's ingenuity. "Can you believe what a dump this place is?"

"I like it," said Meg. "And it's close to our old house, so none of us had to change schools."

"Sure," I said, "but it's so . . . dumpy."

"Shhh," said Georgina. "We're playing."

"Yeah," said Meg. "Why don't you go hang out in your hallway?"

I told Dad I was going for a walk. I grabbed a banana and a piece of toast off the kitchen table and headed out the door of our apartment. A man walked up the stairs toward me. He was brown-skinned, tall, and fleshy. His curly gray hair was piled on top of his head. He wore a striped vest, a floppy bow tie, and a silk bathrobe. A big, shiny mustache covered his top lip. He reminded me of a British detective from the old-fashioned movies Dad liked to watch.

A tube-shaped case about three feet long hung from a strap over the man's shoulder. I assumed it was a telescope and that the man was the astronomer from upstairs. He placed a pair of glasses on his nose. "You're the new neighbor. I felt I would meet you here, just now. And your name—it's a precious name, like gold. Or silver. Ahh! Yes. Silver. And your first name is—no, I'm not that good. But I reckon I got the last name correct."

"How'd you do that?" I said. "My name *is* Silver. Gabe Silver."

"One out of two. Not so bad. I am Doctor Mandrake. I live upstairs from you. One flight closer to the heavens." He spoke with a distinct English accent.

"You're an astronomer?"

"What? No no no. Nothing so pedestrian. I am an *astrologer*. I study stars not for their size or distance, but for what they say about ourselves. Because, and I quote, 'The whole of humanity—past, present, and future—is written on the shiny skin of stars.'"

"That's a cool quote. Who said that?"

"I did. When were you born?"

"December thirtieth."

"Capricorn. Of course. The mighty goat of the sea. And where?"

"Right here. I mean, in Tacoma. Saint Joseph Hospital."

"And what year?"

I told him.

He pulled out a worn booklet and thumbed through it. He stopped at a page and began nodding. "My young Sea Goat, you are within spitting distance of a most particular day. Not today. No no no. My guess is that today will be boring. Today will be for lying on your bed and staring at the ceiling. But tomorrow. Tomorrow, young Sea Goat, will be most particular. A razor's-edge day. The line of decision will be *just that fine*. One millimeter—nay, one micron!—to the east, and all is doom. One micron to the west, and all—all is glory."

"You make it sound pretty serious."

"It will be quite serious. I am certain of it. The question is, will it be good? Let me give you a warning." He put his mouth right next to my ear. I could hear him breathing. He said, "Don't lose your soul."

TUG-OF-WAR

DON'T LOSE YOUR SOUL, Doctor Mandrake had said. I hadn't spent a lot of time thinking about souls—mine or anyone else's.

Dear Reader, that was about to change.

I continued downstairs to the entryway. From Jimmy Hyde's apartment, I could hear what I guessed was Hawaiian music, because every now and then I would hear an *aloha* and a *mahalo* in the lyrics. Jimmy Hyde didn't look like a Hawaiian-music kind of guy.

I walked out to the sidewalk and stared back at the Bright House. It really was a dump. It didn't matter if I was grateful, like Dad wanted me to be. I could dress up like a cheerleader and shake pom-poms at the place and it would still look like a dump.

I walked around the building. On the top floor, I could see Doctor Mandrake bustling about in his apartment with his tube. Below him, Georgina and Meg wrestled against a window, fighting over Georgina's customized Barbie. I looked through my bedroom window and saw my Ferrari poster on the wall, then turned the corner to the back of the building.

A girl with short black hair stared down at me from a second-floor window. She wore a black dress and black makeup around her eyes. She saw me, then ran her finger across her neck, as if she were threatening to slit my throat. She must have been the girl with the sick mom. Her name was Joanna Sedley, but I didn't know that yet.

I kept walking, eager to get out of the girl's line of sight. I turned around the far side of the building and looked up at a window on the corner. It must have been a different room of the girl's apartment. A woman stood there with a scarf on her head and a sad look on her face. *The sick mom.* I stared at her until I walked right into Jimmy Hyde.

"Oh. Sorry," I said. Jimmy Hyde had been looking up at the woman, too. Now he gawked at me, his mostly toothless mouth open. He held a notebook in one hand and a pencil in the other. He quickly jammed both inside his jacket and hurried away without a word.

I didn't think much about it then. But months later, Dear Reader, I'd remember that moment.

I turned the corner to the front of the building. A family that must have been the Brackleys was unloading matching sets of luggage from the back of a new Cadillac Escalade. Seventy-five grand, just for the base model. I bet this one was closer to ninety. I wasn't a big Cadillac fan, but I had to admit, it was quite a car. Black and shiny and about the size of an aircraft carrier. *Why would anyone who could afford a car like that live in a building like this?*

The Brackley dad walked inside before I could get a good look at him. The mom backed out of the hatch of the car, butt first. She wore a checked suit dress and high heels. Her hair was blond. Huge sunglasses covered her eyes. She looked like a movie star. Or maybe more like a former movie star. She pulled a giant suitcase out of the car. It landed on the sidewalk with a thunk. "Lancaster! Come and carry this for Mama. . . ." The woman stood on the sidewalk, hands on her hips, and looked around. "Lanny!"

A boy I assumed was Lancaster walked out from behind Dad's old Honda Civic, dressed in khaki pants and a blue suit jacket. He nodded toward Dad's car. "Take a look at this piece of junk," he said.

"Lancaster, where were you?" said the woman.

"Right here the whole time. I could hear you yelling at me."

"I wasn't yelling *at* you, sweetie," said the woman. "I was yelling *for* you. Lancaster, Lancaster, rah rah rah. *For you.* Now be a dear and bring Mama's suitcase upstairs."

"I gotta get my own stuff. Just pay Alejandro to do it."

"Lanny, don't argue with Mama. Just take my bag up."

"Not a chance. I know what that thing weighs." Lancaster grabbed a backpack out of the Cadillac and walked into the building.

The woman shifted her glare in my direction. "What are you looking at?"

I shrugged. "I think I'm your neighbor. You need some help?"

"Would you mind?"

I grabbed her suitcase and began rolling it toward the doors of the Bright House. I had to drag it up to the second story one stair at a time. By the time I reached the second-floor landing I was sweating, but the movie-star woman kept saying, "Look at how strong you are. And such a gentleman." That kept me going.

I rolled the suitcase to her door, then pointed across the hall. "We live here. Like I said. Neighbors."

"You look about Lancaster's age. Maybe the two of you can be friends. Heaven knows he could use one." She slipped into her apartment and closed the door.

The next morning was Monday. I went back outside to wait for Dad to take me to school. His car—the rusty old Honda Civic—was the key proof in my argument that grown-ups hate cars. I couldn't understand why Dad would choose to drive such a pile of junk. Cars cost money. And we didn't have any money. I got that. But if we had to drive something old, why couldn't it be an old sports car? Or an old convertible? Or even an old truck?

I almost leaned against the car while I waited, but caught myself just in time. If anyone touched the Honda, the paint would flake off, like car dandruff.

I thought about what Doctor Mandrake had said—that this would be a razor's-edge day. "Don't lose your soul," he'd said.

Dad and the girls appeared, and off we went in the Honda in a cloud of smoke.

Most of the morning passed without incident. No razors. No edges.

Between math and social studies, I got a text from Mom asking me to stop by Dave's Cheese Shop on the way home and pick up some cheese called *mizithra* for the spaghetti with browned butter she was planning for dinner. She said she'd already called the shop and would pay later, which was good, since I only had a dollar in my pocket.

At lunch, I grabbed a tray in the cafeteria and loaded it up with a foil-wrapped burrito, Tater Tots, and a carton of chocolate milk. I took a swig of chocolate milk and was looking around for Henry when the girl from the Bright House grabbed my tray.

Wait—since when did she go to my school? I looked her over.

She had short black hair, dark eye makeup, a black dress, and black boots. Even her lipstick was black.

I was definitely looking into the face of my neighbor.

"Let go," I said.

The girl glared at me.

"What is your problem?" I said.

"You are."

"Seriously. Let go."

"Make me." She smiled, just a tiny bit. The smile made her scarier. The kids around us started to notice.

I pulled on my tray again. But she held on just as tightly.

What was I supposed to do? Have a tug-of-war with this girl? She was no bigger than me, so I figured I could probably win, but it would make a huge scene. And I wanted to eat my lunch, not pick it up off the floor.

The crowd grew around us until at least thirty kids were watching. The girl pulled harder on the tray.

"What is your problem?" I said again, almost shouting.

"What is your problem?" she mimicked.

"Let go of my tray!"

"Let go of my tray!"

"Let go!"

"I'll let go if you move out!" She released her grip just as I jerked backwards. I fell to the ground. My lunch flew

through the air, Tater Tots hitting me in the face and scattering on the floor. The carton of chocolate milk landed right on my belt buckle. Milk poured all over my pants. The crowd of kids gasped, then laughed.

"Looks like you wet your pants," said the girl as she turned to leave. The crowd laughed again, then drifted away.

Henry ran over and picked up my burrito. "I think you can still eat this, but your Tots are history. What happened?"

"*That* happened." I pointed at the girl in black.

Henry said, "The goth girl?"

"She lives in my building."

"Ohhh. *That's* what she meant."

"Huh?"

"When she yelled 'Move out!' at you. Geez, you've got her at home and at school. That stinks. I guess she just started here today. I heard she went to Headley Academy before she came here."

"I bet they expelled her," I said.

"Yeah. She's mean," said Henry. "I think she was bullying you."

"Shut up, Henry. She was not bullying me."

"It's tricky when a girl bullies you—"

"She's not bullying me."

"But if she is, what can you do? I mean, you can't fight her. Can you? Maybe you can. I don't know. You should probably tell someone. Hey, are you gonna eat this burrito?"

"We gotta go to class."

"Yeah, but can I have your burrito? And did you know it looks like you wet your pants?"

By the end of the day, kids at school were calling me Chocolate Pants, which is about the stupidest name in the world. I mean, if you're gonna make fun of a kid, at least use a little imagination.

I COME INTO POSSESSION
OF THE BOTTLE

"CHEER UP," said Henry as we walked home from school. "In a few days, everyone will forget about it."

"Easy for you to say."

"Okay, maybe a few months. Hey, how about we go to the batting cage and hit some balls. Maybe it'll take your mind off your—you know—your new nickname."

"I can't. I have to go to the stupid cheese shop for my mom."

"The what?"

"The cheese shop."

"There's a shop? For cheese?"

"Yup. Dave's Cheese Shop."

"And all they sell is cheese?"

"Yes."

"Can I come?"

Henry followed me to Dave's, which was about halfway between school and home.

"I bet I've walked past this place a million times," said

Henry. "How did I never notice it before?" We walked in and Henry sniffed the air. "This is the greatest place I've ever seen. Look at all these glorious cheeses. Check this one out. Ticklemore. I wanna try some Ticklemore. There's a Gorgonzola—I know that one. Oh man, it smells awesome in here. It's so—so cheesy."

I saw Dave behind the counter, dressed in his white apron. I had to look at my phone to remember the name of the cheese Mom wanted, then told Dave I was there for some mizithra.

"For Mrs. Silver. I got it right here. The last piece in the store." Dave pulled a wedge of white cheese out from a glass case and began wrapping it in white paper. A bell chimed. The door opened behind me.

An old man approached the counter in a cloud of smoke.

"Hey, you can't smoke that in here," said Dave.

The man kept sucking on a cigar. He blew a huge puff of smoke toward the ceiling. He nodded at the wedge of mizithra that Dave was wrapping up. "Is that what I think it is?"

"Mizithra," said Dave, "but it's the last of it. You need to take that cigar outside."

"It's already sold, then?" said the old man.

"I told you it was."

"I'll give you twenty dollars for it."

"It's only four ninety-five, but I already sold it to Mrs. Silver. I'm not gonna ask you again about the cigar."

The man reached into his pocket, then said, "I wish you would sell it to me." He smiled a shaky smile. "Fifty dollars?"

42.

"Say what?" said Dave.

"Seventy-five," said the man.

"Whoa."

"Hey," I said. "You already promised that to me."

"I know, kid, but look. It's been a slow day. And your mom hasn't even paid for it yet. Sorry. How about I give you some nice Timberdoodle on the house?"

"Make it Ticklemore," said Henry.

Dave gave Henry a big chunk of Ticklemore. He handed the mizithra to the old man. The man pulled out a fat money clip and peeled off four twenties. "Keep the change." He turned to me. "Sorry son, but when one person wins, another one loses. If it makes you feel better, this little wedge of cheese was my very last wish." He blew another cloud of smoke and went out the door.

That's when I saw the Ferrari.

"Henry, do you see what I see?" I ran outside just as the man was putting his key into the driver's door of a bright red 430. Henry followed on my heels.

I said, "Is this yours?"

"It is," said the man. "Do you know it?"

"Do I know it? I worship it."

"You might not want to do that. Do you recognize the year?"

"No, but they only made these from 2004 to 2009, so it's in there. I'd guess this one is an oh-eight."

"You know your cars," said the old man.

"I know Ferraris. This one's my favorite." I rattled off a half dozen facts I knew about the car.

"What is your name?" said the man.

"Gabe. Gabe Silver."

"Well, Gabe Silver, you like my car. You share my taste in cheeses. Perhaps . . ."

"Perhaps what?"

"Perhaps you're the one. And perhaps I should tell you." He dropped the cigar to the street and ground it out under his shoe. "Do you want to know how I came to be rich?"

I nodded.

"I've needed to tell someone for many years. I've cheated the Devil for far too long." The old man sighed. "I don't have a job. I have something much better than a job."

"Which is?"

"I have a secret."

"And it got you this?"

The man laughed. "I have never told a—a soul. However, today is a special day. A particular day."

"Particular how?"

"Today is the last day I toy with the Devil. I'm done. I gambled. I won, in a sense. Now it is time to stop betting."

The old man reached into the pocket of his jacket and pulled out a little bottle. It was white, but other colors danced across its surface. If I'd had to guess, I would have said it was carved from stone. It stood maybe five inches tall at the most. A matching stopper protruded from the top.

"This is my secret."

"That? What's it supposed to be? Some kind of magic potion?"

"Not a bad guess. But there's no potion in here. There's a tiny imp."

"A what?"

"An imp. Some might call him a genie, but that evokes images of fairy tales and *The Arabian Nights*. This is nothing like that. Others might call him by older names. A fiend. A genius. A djinn."

"Okay. This is weird. I'm gonna leave now."

"Wait!" The old man grabbed me by the sleeve. "Please. I need you to hear my story."

I pulled myself free. "I really think I should go."

"I'm not asking you to do anything. Just—just listen."

Henry pulled on my other sleeve. "Gabe, I think we should get out of here."

"Just wait a sec," I said. "Okay. I'm listening."

The old man took a deep breath and steadied himself against his car. He said, "The tiny one who lives inside, he is no bigger than your thumb. He is the imp—a servant of the Other. Whatever I wish for, the imp makes sure I get it. This morning—this last morning of all mornings—I wished my very last wish. A simple thing. Just a bit of cheese."

"Cheese? Wouldn't you wish for riches? For a kazillion dollars or something?"

He patted the red roof of the Ferrari. "I did that already. Riches, houses, cars. All I had to do was ask. You don't believe me. Of course you don't. But it's true."

"I'm gonna go now," I said. "Nice car."

The old man laughed. "It's funny. I've been petrified my secret would get out. That someone would discover the means to my great success. And now I confess and you don't believe me." He laughed again. "I could have been forthright all along." He rubbed the side of the bottle with his thumb, then looked at me. "And today is the day. I think that you should be the next."

"The next what?"

"The next owner of the bottle."

"Why?"

"Because you seem like a good person, but not too good. And it's time to strike a bargain. Come sit in my car with me."

"Serious?"

"Very."

Henry said, "Don't do that, Gabe. You know you shouldn't do that."

"Yeah, but . . . it's a Ferrari. I'm gonna sit in it. Just for a minute." I walked to the other side of the car and opened the door. I slid onto the soft leather seat but left the door open. "It's nice," I said.

"I'm going to tell you the complete truth so that you know what you may be getting into," the man said. He cleared his throat, making a sound like a pebble rattling in a rusty can. "Approximately one hundred and fifty years ago, this bottle of mine was brought to the earth by—well, by the Devil himself, as a way to capture a human soul. And he will capture one with it, someday. After all, riches, cars, wishes—what are these to the Devil, when an eternal soul is on the other side of the balance?" He held out the bottle. "This was first purchased by John D. Rockefeller in 1870—"

"Rocky who?"

"Rockefeller. John D. Famous for his unfathomable wealth. Sort of the Bill Gates of his day, I suppose. Rockefeller purchased the bottle for one thousand dollars."

"From the Devil? The real Devil?"

"The real one. Make no bones about that. It made him incredibly wealthy. People thought he got rich from oil, but this was the real cause. This bottle. Since then, it's been owned by many of the richest people—Weyerhaeuser, Edison, Walton, Buffett. I bought it from Mr. Buffett myself, near a corn field in Omaha, Nebraska. I've owned it for nearly seven years, and it's made me very rich. And very tired. And very lonely, too. I want to be rid of it. I need to be, if I can manage to part with it."

"That doesn't make sense. If it really made you rich, why would you ever want to give it up?"

Henry was leaning against the passenger door. "Let's just go, Gabe."

"Just a sec. I want to hear his answer, if he has one."

The old man smiled. "I have an answer. And the rules of the bottle say that I'm required to tell you . . . to tell you how this works. To explain the whole deal. Because wishes don't come for free. When one person wins, another loses. And— and the bottle came from the Devil, so there's a catch. If you die with it in your possession, the Devil claims your soul."

A chill ran over me. "Meaning what?"

"Meaning your soul belongs to the Devil. For all eternity."

"But you're still alive. So he never claimed yours. You've gotten off scot-free."

His eyes grew wide. "Scot-free? I'd never pretend such a thing. The weight of ownership—yes, that's the right word, the *weight*—it can be heavy. What if I were to die today? What would become of me? Of my soul?"

"Not much of a sales pitch. This is how you're gonna try to sell it to me?"

"It is. You must know. It is required that you know. And I am indeed trying to sell it to you. I've waited too long. And I do so want to avoid that final bargain."

"Well, I only have one dollar, so you're wasting your time."

The man smiled. "Another sign. I can only take one dollar for it. Or less, but not a penny more. When I bought it years ago from Mr. Buffett, I paid one dollar and one cent. And the rules of the bottle say I must sell it for a loss. If I try to rid myself of it any other way, the bottle will just come back to me. The rules also say that it can't be sold for less than one cent and each transaction must be a whole coin. No half pennies. No decimals. And no wishing to change the rules. At the end of the line, some poor soul will buy it for a penny and end up stuck with the thing." The old man stared at the bottle in his hand. "And then the Devil will get his due."

Henry grabbed at my sleeve. I waved him off. "Only a dollar? It is a cool looking bottle. And the story is kind of awesome, even if it's just a story."

"It's true," said the man, "and the bottle contains what I said it does. An imp. You need to recognize that as fact. Don't deal with me if you don't realize the true bargain you're making, for good or ill."

I tried to swallow, but my mouth was dry.

"Try it and see, if you still don't believe. Give me your dollar in exchange for the bottle, then wish for your money back. If a dollar is not returned to you, then I will buy the bottle back from you for ninety-nine pennies and you'll only be out one cent."

Henry shouted, *"Don't do it, Gabriel. This kind of stuff creeps me out. And you shouldn't be in a stranger's car!"*

I reached my hand into my pocket and pulled out my dollar. I knew it was just a story—there was no way it could be true.

I looked at the bottle in the old man's hand. It probably just caught the light in a funny way, but right then, I thought I saw a shadow flit across its surface, as if something inside of it moved. A chill ran up my back. I shivered, but I handed over my dollar.

"Tell me your name again," said the old man.

"Gabriel Silver. What's yours?"

"Oh, my name doesn't matter. And where are you from?"

"I'm from here. Tacoma."

"Gabriel Silver, from Tacoma, Washington, I take your dollar in exchange for the bottle and the imp."

The old man handed the bottle to me. I swear that as soon as he did so, his face relaxed and he sat a little straighter. "Now wish to have your dollar back in your pocket," he said.

"How?"

"Just wish to the imp. No magic words required. No need to rub the lamp. Just hold the bottle in your hand and wish to the imp."

A big part of me didn't want to do it. Part of me wanted to just drop the bottle and run. But I said, "I wish for my dollar back in my pocket."

"Now feel inside your pocket and see if it's there."

I put my hand into the pocket of my jeans. The pocket was empty. "Sorry. No luck."

"Check again."

"There's nothing in there. I told you, I only had the one dollar." I pulled the pocket inside out to show how empty it was.

A tiny ball of paper fell to the floor of the car. I spread it open. It was a wrinkled one-dollar bill.

"So!" said the old man. "Our deal is done. Make your wishes with great care. No wishing to change the rules or to destroy the bottle. Remember that when one person wins, another one loses. And don't wait too long to sell it. Don't risk dying with it in your possession."

"Or what?"

"Or the Devil will take you."

I climbed out of the car. With a squeal of his tires, he drove away.

I MAKE MY SECOND WISH

"YOU SHOULD GET RID OF THAT THING," said Henry as we walked toward the Bright House. "That old man said it came from the Devil. You don't want to mess around with stuff like that."

"Geez, Henry, you are such a wimp."

"There are just some things that you shouldn't mess around with, and the Devil is one of them."

"It's not real," I said, but as the words came out of my mouth I felt more fragile, more aware of the dangers of the world. I'd never thought about my soul before, or what might become of it when I died. Now, with the bottle in my hand, death seemed more possible. I checked for cars twice before we crossed the Yakima Street Bridge, which ran over a deep, dry gully.

Henry said, "If it's not real, then how come you got your dollar back?"

I shook the feelings from my head. "It was some kind of trick by the old guy. I bet he slipped that tiny, crumpled-up dollar into my pocket. Probably right when he first met us. I bet he did it right when he came in the store."

"Well, if it's not really magical, then you should just throw it off this bridge right now."

"I can't throw it away," I said. "Didn't you hear the old man? If I try to get rid of it without selling it for a loss, it'll just come back to me."

"I thought you said it wasn't real," said Henry. He snatched the bottle from my hand and ran to the railing of the bridge.

"Henry, don't you dare."

"I'm doing you a favor. I'm saving your soul." He threw the bottle as far as he could.

Even for a catcher on a baseball team, Henry had a wicked arm. He wasn't fast. He wasn't the best hitter. But from home plate he could throw out a runner trying to steal second. He threw that bottle like a game was on the line. It sailed through the air, landing down in the gully in a huge mound of blackberry bushes.

"You jerk, Henry." I shoved him.

He stumbled, then ran away from me. "You should be thanking me."

"Get out of here before I punch you."

"You'll thank me someday," he called as he ran across the bridge toward his house.

I climbed down into the gulley and dug through the bushes for half an hour. I scared away half a dozen crows, but found nothing. I cursed Henry every time a blackberry thorn scratched me, then walked home alone.

When I came to the Bright House, I found Doctor

Mandrake pacing up and down the sidewalk. "Finally, young Sea Goat. It's about time you arrived."

"You've been waiting? For me?"

"Yes. Yes I have. Now tell me about your day. I was right, wasn't I? About it being a most particular day. A razor's-edge day."

"It was particular, all right."

"Ah-*ha*! I knew it! I was right! I was right! And I said you had a choice. Did you choose well?"

"I have no idea. Do you mind if I go? I don't really feel like talking right now."

"Just wait a minute, young Sea Goat. I'm not done yet. I have to tell you about the strangest thing that just happened. I came out here to consider the day, to contemplate my relationship to the earth and sun. I was standing like this— arms spread, open to the present, on the best of terms with the world—when a crow dive-bombed me."

"A bird?"

"A black crow. Wings spread, cawing like mad. And—now, this is the important part—it held something in his talons." Doctor Mandrake reached inside his cape. "The crow dropped it. Right at my feet. And I knew—I just knew—it was for you. Nothing valuable. But the thing practically shouted at me, 'Give me to the young Sea Goat!' It's just a trifle, mind you. Now where is it?" He dug through his pockets. "I know I have it somewhere. Ah. Here it is."

Doctor Mandrake held the white bottle in his hand. My breath caught in my throat. "A crow dropped this?"

"It's not much, I know. But sometimes small things can be monumental. And it's got—a certain *vibration* to it. It just shouts energy. Makes one feel wide awake. And it is yours." He swept his cape around him and disappeared into the building.

I looked down at the bottle. It felt heavy in my hand. A shadow flitted across its surface. This time there was no mistaking it. "So you're back," I said. That same chill went down my spine, making me shiver again. Should I make a wish? Or should I get rid of the bottle just as fast as I could? I wondered, just for a moment, if Henry might be right.

Dad stepped out of the apartment building, dressed in his Hasty's Pizza uniform. "Hey, kiddo. How was school?"

"Fine," I mumbled.

"What've you got there?"

I should have told Dad right then, before everything got so crazy. I should have told him the whole story. I didn't. "Doctor Mandrake gave it to me," I said.

"Really? Well, be careful with it. That guy's kind of a whack job. Did you know he's not even a real astronomer? Anyway, I've got to go."

"You're leaving? Now?"

"Time for me to deliver some pizza pies."

"But I need to talk to you."

"We can talk later. I'm gonna be late." He rubbed the top of my head and started for the car.

"Wait!" I said.

"What?"

I looked down at the bottle in my hand. "I wish—I wish you had your old job back," I said.

"Me too, kid." Dad left.

Mrs. Appleyard was leaning against the wall of the Bright House's entryway, staring at me with a cigarette in her mouth. I could hear Jimmy Hyde's radio blaring what sounded like more of that Hawaiian music, while the sounds of Mrs. Hashimoto puttering away came from her door.

"Hey, Ten Cents. How're you all settling in?" said Mrs. Appleyard. Her eyes were on the bottle in my hand.

"Fine, I guess."

"You don't sound very sure."

I shrugged. "Yeah."

"Yeah what?"

"Yeah. I guess I'm not very sure."

"Well now, Ten Cents, you just let Mrs. Appleyard know what she can do to help. I like happy tenants. Happy tenants pay their rent on time. Whatcha got in your hand there?"

"Nothing." I slid the bottle into the pocket of my jeans.

"Nothing, hmm? When they say it's nothing, it's always something. Mr. Appleyard used to get tummy aches. Right in his tummy-tum-tum. I could tell when he had one, cause he'd walk more bent over than usual. So I'd say, 'What's wrong, dear?' He always said, 'Nothing.' And then one day, nothing turned into something."

"Turned into what?"

"Into something that killed him, that's what. Turns out he'd eaten a fish he'd caught. A little bullhead. Swallowed it whole. That bullhead was so fresh that it came back alive in his gut. It swam around in Mr. Appleyard's stomach, eating all his food. While the fish got bigger, Mr. Appleyard starved right to death. Next thing you know, he's taking his final fishing trip in the back of a hearse." She wiped her eyes on the cuff of her bathrobe. "Now I keep his ashes on a bookshelf. And he never made it to Mexico."

"He wanted to visit Mexico?"

"Wanted to move there. To a little fishing village called El Pescadero. That was his dream, Ten Cents. To own a boat and go fishing every day. Instead, he ended up on a bookshelf."

"Why do you keep calling me that?"

"What? Ten Cents? Because you're like a dime, that's why."

"Like a dime?"

"Sure. You're a little Silver."

I went upstairs. In the living room, the carpet was mostly dry and the bucket was gone, but now there was a huge hole torn in the ceiling, exposing the pipes that Alejandro must have repaired.

Mom yelled at me for not bringing home her mizithra, even though I told her it wasn't my fault. I went into my bedroom and lay down on my bed, still holding the bottle in my hand. I wondered how many hands had held it the same way, how many owners had wondered if it was real or not.

About an hour later, I heard Dad come home. I left my room, hoping he'd brought pizza for dinner.

"Why are you here?" said Mom. "I thought you were working a long shift."

"I quit, my dear," said Dad. He took the Hasty's hat from his head and put it on Mom.

"Oh, Johann."

"Oh, Johann? Would you believe Oh Johann got his job back?"

"Got his what?"

"His job. His teaching job. Associate professor. And tenure track at that."

"What are you talking about?"

"Billingsly called me. Said the dean was reading my evaluations and didn't understand how they could have ever let me go. Told Billingsly to track me down. That's what he said. That he was told to *track me down.*" Dad grabbed Mom around the waist. "No more pizza, *señora.* Tonight, we're going out—for tacos!"

"Tacos? Oh, but I made spaghetti. Without mizithra."

"Put it in Tupperware, baby. It's taco night."

They all ran down the stairs together. Mom and the girls laughed and shouted. Dad sang in Spanish. I followed after, one step at a time. I could swear the weight of the bottle pulled me down the stairs. I wondered if I'd be able to eat a taco, because my stomach felt like a whole troupe of acrobats was warming up down there.

I'd made my first wish and it had already come true.

I should be happy, right? I should be ecstatic. Then why did I feel like I was gonna barf?

We jammed into Dad's car. The worn seats still smelled like Hasty's Pizza. Dad turned the key and black smoke puffed out the back.

"Maybe since I got the job, it's time to think about a better car," said Dad.

"We need to get out of this apartment first," said Mom.

"What?" said Georgina. "We're not moving, are we?"

"Yeah," said Meg. "We love it here."

Dad sighed. "No one is moving."

I said, "Dad, you know what car I saw today? A Ferrari 430."

"Nice. A new one?"

"A Ferrari 430, Dad. There are no new ones. They stopped making them in 2009. I saw one. Right here in Tacoma. That's what you should get. You could drive me to school in it. Can you imagine?"

"I was thinking more like a Honda that didn't smoke so much."

"Make sure you get one that still smells like pizza," said Meg. She took a big sniff.

"No one is getting a car," said Mom. "What we need is a house."

"I thought you said we weren't moving," said Georgina.

"He said that. Not me."

"We're not moving," said Dad. "We have too many bills we still need to pay off before we can even think about a house. Besides. I signed a one-year lease."

"A Ferrari 430, Dad. That's what you need."

"What I need right now is a taco."

I reached into my pocket, touching the smooth surface of the bottle. I whispered, "I wish my dad had a Ferrari 430."

A KEY IS DELIVERED

WHEN I OPENED MY EYES THE NEXT MORNING, the first thing I saw was my poster. The Ferrari. I looked out my window, half expecting to see a real one in front of our building, but Dad's old Honda still sat down there, slowly disintegrating by the curb. Right behind it was a black Volkswagen Beetle. No Ferrari in sight.

When Dad dropped me off at school, the same black VW Beetle pulled up behind us. Out stepped the new girl. Joanna Something. She glared at me. I glared back, then noticed the car's driver—the pale, thin woman with dark eyes and a scarf tied around her head whom I'd seen in the window.

Dad nodded toward the Beetle. "Don't they live in our building?"

"Yes."

"A new friend for you, then," Dad said. "I'm going to ask the mom if she'd like us to drive her daughter to school. We could carpool."

"What? No!" I said.

"Why not?"

"Because—because she's weird, Dad. Don't—"

"Oh, come on, Gabe. Give the girl a chance. She's just a bit goth. My understanding is that goth girls are cool. And you could use some cool friends. Not that Henry isn't—you know—cool."

Dad walked toward the Volkswagen. I hurried to the school building. When I stepped inside, someone shoved me from behind. I stumbled forward and fell.

Joanna stood over me. "Why's your dad talking to my mom?" I tried to stand up, but she pushed me down with a black boot. "Why's he talking to her?"

"I don't know. He wants to start a car pool or something."

"No!"

"It's not my idea."

"Stay out. Stay out of my life!" She stomped away.

I got up and noticed Henry leaning against his locker, watching the whole thing. Without a word, he turned and disappeared down the hall.

I managed to avoid Joanna throughout the day. I'd brought my own lunch—I wanted nothing to do with trays—and I sat in the corner of the cafeteria with my back against the wall. That way Joanna couldn't sneak up on me. Henry sat by himself at our old table, poking at his Jell-O with his plastic fork.

After lunch, Henry and Joanna were both in my language arts class, and my assigned seat was right next to Henry. I was still mad at him for throwing away my bottle.

I guess he was mad at me, too, because we both turned our desks away from each other.

Our language arts teacher, Miss Kratz, asked Joanna to come to the whiteboard and write a prepositional phrase. Joanna didn't move.

"Joanna, I know you heard me. Can you please come on up?" Miss Kratz was about fifty years old, I guess, but she dressed in the same brands of clothes as some of my classmates.

Joanna said, "Why?"

"Why what, dear?"

"Why do I have to come forward? Can't you just write one?"

"It would certainly be easier. I could do the whole class that way and all of you could just stay home. Unfortunately, that's not the way this whole teaching thing works. You actually have to learn something."

Joanna sighed, then shuffled up to the front. She picked up a marker and wrote *out the door* on the board.

"Good," said Miss Kratz. "*Out* is the preposition, and *door* is the object, so *out the door* is a prepositional phrase. Now can you make it into a sentence?"

Joanna added four words to the front. The new sentence read *I want to run out the door.*

"You and me both, honey," said Miss Kratz. "But there's still more than a month until summer. We'll both try to make it. Now go back to your seat."

At the end of the school day, I started walking home by myself. Before I turned the corner at the end of the block, I looked back. I could see Henry watching me from the school steps. When he saw me, I reached into my pocket and pulled out the bottle to show him he hadn't won. He turned away.

Who needed Henry? So what if we'd known each other since first grade? So what if we hung out seven days a week? Half the time we were together he drove me nuts. And if I wanted a new friend, I could get one.

I reached into my pocket and touched the bottle. "I wish I had a new friend."

When I got to the Bright House, Mrs. Appleyard was sitting out front in a rusty lawn chair, smoking a cigarette. "All alone, Ten Cents? You a lone wolf?"

"A what?"

"You a loner? You like to go it on your own?"

"I don't think so. I mean, not really. I like hanging out with friends."

"Where are they?"

"Who? My—my friends? I don't know. I'm kind of, you know, in between right now."

"A lone wolf." She howled, but ended it with a coughing fit. "I'm the same way, since Mr. Appleyard left me." She laughed. "We always end up alone. You know why?"

I shook my head no.

"Because people always leave you. Always. Says so right in our wedding vows: 'Till death do us part.' They get you ready for the parting right when they do the connecting. And that *till death* bit—that's a best-case scenario."

Mrs. Appleyard flicked her cigarette butt into the weeds. It smoldered there. I wondered for a second if it might catch the weeds on fire, until Mrs. Appleyard reached with a foot and ground it out. She lifted her foot, then ground it out some more. She said, "Don't want to start any fires. Least not yet. Hey, I almost forgot. Tell your dad there was some guy here earlier looking for him. A lawyer type. Had some fat envelope with him, but he wouldn't leave it. I asked."

I went inside. Upstairs, I was fishing for the key to our apartment when the door across the hall opened up. The Brackley kid—Lancaster—stepped out. He wore a pair of huge headphones.

I pointed to my ear and said, "What are you listening to?"

"Huh?"

I repeated the question. He pulled off the headphones and named a band I'd never heard of. I wondered if Lancaster was the answer to my wish for a new friend. "Wanna play some video games?" I asked.

He shrugged. "I guess."

"Your place or mine?"

"How big's your TV?"

I held my hands apart. "About this big."

"Then let's use mine."

I followed Lancaster into his apartment, but could only step inside a few feet before a chair blocked my path. The apartment was jammed from one wall to another with furniture—carved wooden tables, rich leather chairs, and sofas. The tiny living room must have had enough seating for twenty people, but no room to walk.

Gold-framed paintings covered the walls. I mean they were *covered.* The paintings fitted together on the walls like a jigsaw puzzle, with only an occasional smoke detector added into the mix. Extra paintings sat on the floor, jammed between the chairs and couches.

"Watch that wall," Lancaster said. He clicked on a remote. A projector mounted to the ceiling hummed to life. A screen rolled down from the top of the wall. Lancaster passed me a game controller and climbed over one couch in order to reach another. "Sit anywhere you want," he said. I climbed my way over two sofas and a chair—my feet never touching the ground—until I reached a big leather recliner. "Good choice," said Lancaster. "If you want to recline, just use the buttons."

I settled into the chair and hit a button. The chair hummed and started to lean back, then stopped against another chair. There was no room to recline. Lancaster shrugged. "Trust me. It's cool when it works."

A zombie game I wasn't allowed to play at home was projected onto the giant screen. Lancaster turned up the volume so loud it rattled the whole apartment.

"Pretty cool, huh?"

"It's awesome." I put my feet on the arm of the chair in front of mine.

The bedroom door opened and a woman stumbled out. I didn't recognize her at first. Her hair was messy, her face pale, and her eyes looked tired and small. She wore a bathrobe over her pajamas. "Lanny, turn that garbage down, would you? Mama is trying to sleep."

"It's three in the afternoon," said Lancaster. "It's about time Mama got up."

"Mama had a late night last night and still needs a little nappy. Turn it off before I—" She spotted me. "Lanny, you could have told me you had company. Is this—are you the boy from the building? Lanny, what's your friend's name?"

Lancaster kept playing. "I don't know. Ask him."

"Gabe," I said.

She tightened her bathrobe and smoothed down her hair. "Nice to see you again, Gabe. I must look a fright. Lanny, can you please turn down the volume? Just a little for Mama? Show your new friend that you can be a nice boy."

Lancaster rolled his eyes and hit the pause button. "Fine," he said. He clicked the volume down a few levels, then looked at his mother. "Happy now?"

"Thank you, dear." She disappeared back into the bedroom.

Lancaster clicked the volume back up. "Watch out. You're about to get fragged." Lancaster's avatar shot mine as Mrs. Brackley's words echoed through my head. "Your new friend," she'd said.

This could be awesome. I'd get access to his giant TV. Then I remembered: I could wish for my own giant TV. I could wish for anything.

I peppered Lancaster with questions while we played. He was a year ahead of me in school. He went to Charles Wright Academy. His dad ran something called a hedge fund. I asked Lancaster what it was. Lancaster said, "Volatile."

"What's that mean?"

"It means sometimes we're rich and sometimes we're less rich. That's what Goody says."

"Who's Goody?"

Lancaster nodded toward the bedroom door. "Stepmom. She's volatile, too."

"How long have you lived here?"

"This time? About two months. But this is our third time in this dump. Before this we lived in Old Town. With a pool. And a pool house. I had the pool house all to myself."

"Yeah. I miss our old place, too."

"Where was it?"

"Twelfth and Holly."

"Twelfth, huh?"

"Meaning what?"

"Just that my dad says nothing counts on the south side of twenty-first."

Our conversation stopped because Lancaster didn't ask anything else about me. We shot zombies for a while, then I said I should probably get going. I mean, I like shooting zombies as much as the next guy. And I guess it was good to be doing it with someone. But it wasn't the same as hanging out with Henry. No jokes. No laughing. Just shooting.

Lancaster mumbled goodbye and kept playing. I climbed to the edge of the furniture and let myself out.

I walked to the window at the end of the hallway and looked down to the street below. I saw a gray sedan parked there, then saw Dad's old Honda sputter to a stop behind it. I went down to meet him.

As I stepped outside, a bald man in a suit slid out of the sedan. He approached Dad. "Johann Silver?"

"That's me," said Dad.

"To clarify, you are Johann Silver, of 601 North K Street, Unit 202, Tacoma, Washington."

"Yes, but—"

"And your birth date is November 13?"

"Umm, yes."

"Then this is for you." The bald man held out a thick envelope.

Dad's hands stayed at his sides. "I'd like to know what this is about."

"It's about your welfare. Trust me. No bad news here. I'm an attorney. I represent a Mr. Shoreby. Does that name mean anything to you?"

"Shoreby? Never heard of him."

"Well, it doesn't really matter. His will very specifically named you."

"His will?"

"Yes. Unfortunately, Mr. Shoreby died yesterday. Unfortunately for him, at least." The bald man reached into the envelope and pulled out a stack of paper. "For you, I'd say the right word is *fortunately*. You just need to sign right here."

Dad crossed his arms. "I—I still want to know what I'm signing."

The bald man sighed. "A car. Shoreby left you a car. Nothing scary. Nothing complicated. Just sign the paper and I'll give you the keys. Car will be delivered tomorrow."

"What kind of car?"

"If you don't sign the paper, you'll never know."

Dad frowned, but grabbed the pen, glanced over a few pages, and signed. The bald man took the signed paper, then handed Dad the rest of the envelope. "Keys are inside. Might want to find a garage to store it in. This ain't the type of car you park on the street." The bald man walked a few steps, then stopped and turned. "There is one more thing.

A small stipulation. Shoreby's will requires you to attend his service."

"You mean his funeral? But I've never met the man."

"Doesn't matter. Page three, paragraph two. You and your eldest child. Tomorrow at three-thirty. Peat Funeral Home on Sixth." The man left.

Dad and I walked back inside. "You need to go with me tomorrow," said Dad. "You're my oldest kid."

"Fine. But what kind of a car is it?"

Dad began sorting through the papers as he climbed the stairs. "I don't know. All this legal mumbo jumbo. I've never even heard of anyone named Shoreby. I mean, does that sound even slightly familiar to you?"

"Never heard of him," I said. "Where's the key?"

"Right here. But it doesn't say the kind of car."

Dad handed the key to me. The key had a red top. In the center of the top was a yellow square. Inside the yellow square was a tiny black horse. I nearly fainted.

"Dad—"

"What?"

"Do you know what this is?"

"What? It's a key."

"You know what kind of car it's for?"

"I already told you I don't know. All these papers."

"Dad, it's a Ferrari key."

A DEATH IS ANNOUNCED

THE NEXT MORNING WAS SATURDAY. I woke up early and ran outside, but no car was there yet.

Dad and I had looked through the envelope. He was right. It was full of legal mumbo jumbo. There was a highlighted section of the will, showing Dad's inheritance. It listed this Mr. Shoreby and his red Ferrari. It didn't say what kind of Ferrari it was. And it didn't say who Mr. Shoreby was.

I heard a door open behind me. I assumed it was Dad. "It's not here yet," I said.

"What's not here yet, you little geek?"

I recognized the voice of Joanna. I didn't turn around. "None of your business."

"It's my business if it's in my building."

"It's not your building. Lots of people live here."

"It's more mine than yours. I was here first."

My hand touched the bottle in my pocket. I thought, just for a second, about wishing for Joanna to disappear.

Poof. Just one little wish and she would cease to exist. "You better watch the way you treat me."

Joanna laughed. "Or what? You gonna beat me up? Or tell your mommy on me?"

My hand went back to the bottle. "You seriously better watch it. Just because your mom is sick doesn't make it okay for you to—"

Joanna grabbed me by the collar and hauled me to my feet. "What did you just say?"

"I—I meant—"

"Never mention my mom again." Her eyes were wide, her nostrils flaring. "She has nothing to do with you. I have nothing to do with you. We are not your business." She shoved me back down to the ground. "Stay—out—of—my—life!"

I sat on the curb by myself for the next hour, feeling alone. I thought about hanging out with Lancaster—after all, he was my new friend, wasn't he? But I didn't really want his company.

A flatbed truck turned the corner onto our street, with a car on its back, under a cloth cover. I texted Dad.

The whole family came outside. Mrs. Appleyard walked across the street from Hank's. "This is about the envelope from yesterday, isn't it?" she said to me. I nodded. "Things

are looking up for the Silvers. Heard your Dad got a job. Now he gets a car. Maybe I should raise your rent."

"Don't even think about it," said Mom.

"Didn't know you were listening," said Mrs. Appleyard. "I was just kidding, of course. I don't raise rents until December. That's how Mr. Appleyard did it. That's how I do it, in honor of his dear memory. Gotta stay on the schedule. The schedule is everything."

The truck driver rolled the car to the ground and drove away, leaving us all staring at this package parked on the curb. Out of the corner of my eye, I saw Joanna watching us from an upstairs window.

"Well, I'd say it's about time we unwrapped our present," said Dad. "Who wants to help?" We all rushed forward. In a whoosh, the cover came off, revealing shiny red paint and gleaming chrome.

"It's a beauty," said Dad.

"I don't believe it," I said. "It's a 430."

"Is that a good thing?"

"It's the best thing. It's the very best thing on—on the whole planet." I touched the bottle in my pocket and shouted, *"Oh, thank you, thank you, thank you!"*

Dad said, "I'd say you're welcome, but I didn't have much to do with it. I suppose we should thank Mr. Shoreby, whoever that is."

"Why would someone you don't even know leave you a car like this?" said Mom. "It doesn't make any sense."

"Who cares if it makes sense," I said. "It's beautiful."

"There's got to be a catch," said Mom. "There's always a catch."

Meg and Georgina begged to go for a ride. "Oh, I don't think we should drive it," said Dad.

I spun around and stared at Dad. "What? What do you mean?"

"Well, what's a car like this worth?"

"I don't know. A good one—with all original stuff—maybe two hundred."

"Two hundred what?"

"Two hundred thousand."

"Dollars? Then we are definitely not driving it. We're going to sell it. I'll find a dealer who will come and pick it up. That's money we could use to get back into a house."

I felt sick to my stomach. "Dad—Dad, you—you can't be serious. You're not serious, are you? I mean, this is—somebody died so you could have this car."

Dad laughed. "I don't think that's the reason he died, Gabe."

"But you're supposed to take me to school in it. That was the whole point!"

"The whole point of what?" said Mom, narrowing her eyes at me.

"Of—of—you know." I gulped.

"Of what?"

"Of having a car like this. I mean, what's the point of getting a Ferrari if all you're going to do is sell it?"

Dad said, "The point is that it's practically worth a whole house, Gabe. We could move out of this building and into our own place."

"Move out?" said Meg.

"We don't want to move," said Georgina. "We like living in an apartment. Apartments are awesome. People above ya—"

"And people below ya," said Meg.

Dad said, "It's not a practical car for our family, Gabe. It only has two seats. Besides, I agreed to start taking that girl—Joanna—to school with you. Make things a little easier on them. Here, help me put the cover back on it."

"No!" I shouted. I laid my body against the car. "You can't get rid of it. It's not right."

"Then I'll just cover you up, too," said Dad. He flung the cover over my head.

Tears started running down my face as I climbed out from underneath.

"Gabe—" said Dad. He tried to put his hand on my shoulder.

"Don't touch me," I said.

I ran up to our apartment. Joanna was leaning against the wall outside our door.

"Poor baby," she said. "Didn't Daddy take you for a drive in his new car?"

"Shut up," I said.

"What's eating you?" Joanna said.

"Seriously. Just shut up."

Joanna smiled.

"And stop smiling."

"But I like seeing you so unhappy," she said.

"I hate living in this stupid building."

"Then move."

"The sooner the better," I said.

"I couldn't agree more."

I went inside and looked around our crappy apartment. There was still a hole in the ceiling where Alejandro had torn it open to fix the leaky pipes.

I was so mad at Dad, my hands were shaking. I thrust one into my pocket and pulled out the bottle. I wanted to do something. For a second, I thought about throwing the bottle across the room. Instead, I wished.

"I wish for—for fifty thousand dollars. I wish for the hole in the stupid ceiling to be fixed. And I wish for—for—I wish for a—for a—for a hot tub!"

I don't know why I said it. I wanted something crazy. Something extravagant, like Lancaster's giant TV. If I couldn't have the Ferrari, then by God, we'd have a hot tub instead.

I didn't have time to think about it. There was a knock on the door. I opened it, half expecting a delivery man to ask where I wanted the hot tub, but it was Doctor Mandrake. He was wearing a blue silk robe over shiny gold pajamas. His eyes were red. His chin was unshaven. He had the morning newspaper folded under his arm.

"Ahh, young Sea Goat. I was hoping to find you here. Very good. Very good. The strangest thing. Since we spoke the other day I have not slept a wink. Not a single minute of sleep. There is a great disturbance in the energy of this building, and I can tell it is connected to *you*. But is it *you*, the personhood of you? Or is it that blasted bottle?"

Doctor Mandrake yawned. "Poor me. I am quite sensitive to shifts in the energy fields, you see. And this one—this field—is concurrent with Capricorn in midheaven. That is your house, you see. It is unique to you—your astral fingerprint, you might say. But it may also be connected to the object that entered under the apex of that house. May I see it? The bottle?"

I pulled it from my pocket and nervously handed it to Mandrake.

Mandrake asked me to hold his newspaper while he examined the bottle. "Ah-ha. Yes. It practically *excretes* energy, does it not? This is the culprit, I tell you. This thing."

"What are you looking for?" I asked.

"I don't know, I don't know. Perhaps . . . hmmm . . ." Mandrake continued mumbling under his breath. While he turned the bottle in every direction, I unfolded the newspaper. Down in the corner of the front page was a small headline: TACOMA'S RICHEST CITIZEN DIES. Underneath it was a name: Shoreby.

Here's what the article said:

> Mr. Shoreby, the reclusive philanthropist of Tacoma with no known first name, was found dead in his home Tuesday night. Early medical reports failed to identify the cause of death.
>
> Shoreby was known both for his charitable giving and for his mysterious past. While he had little contact with the community, he donated millions of dollars to local causes, particularly in support of parks, libraries, and the Shoreby Wing of Tacoma General Hospital.

Shoreby had no known family members and, as of this writing, little is known of his history or how he made his fortune. Private services will be held at Peat Funeral Home in Tacoma. Shoreby's attorney was contacted for information regarding the Shoreby estate, but he declined to comment.

"Something catch your eye?" asked Doctor Mandrake.

"Huh?" I could barely speak. An overwhelming thought pressed on my brain. *Was Mr. Shoreby the man who had sold me the bottle?* And then, half a second later, another thought pushed that one out of the way: *Had Mr. Shoreby died because of my wish? Had I killed him by wishing?*

Mandrake grabbed my arm. "Look," he said. "You see these two tiny marks on the bottom of the bottle? These were carved there by the maker. They are hard to decipher. Get me a piece of paper, would you?"

I grabbed a scrap of lined notebook paper from my bedroom. Mandrake pressed it against the bottom of the bottle. He pulled a stub of a pencil from his robe pocket and rubbed it against the paper until two stick-figure marks appeared.

The first looked like a bird—maybe a falcon—but with a human head. The one next to that was a man kneeling. His hands were behind his back and tied with rope.

"Fascinating, fascinating," said Mandrake. "These look quite old. Perhaps from a pictographic society."

"A what?"

"Oh, you know. A society that used symbols instead of an alphabet. Like ancient Egypt and their hieroglyphs." Mandrake handed me the paper, but held on to the bottle. "I know I gave this object to you," he said, "but would you mind if I borrowed it for a while?"

This bottle had given my dad a job. It had given us a Ferrari. It might have also killed Mr. Shoreby. I knew the bottle would come back to me.

"Take it," I said.

I VIEW A DEAD BODY

WHILE DAD AND I WERE GETTING READY for the funeral, I found the envelope the lawyer had left. I dug the Ferrari key out and when Dad and I went outside, I held it out to him.

Dad said, "Put that away, Gabe. We're not driving that car."

"Why not, Dad? The funeral home's only about a mile away. It'd just be a little drive."

"Yeah, and one car pulls out and the Ferrari is destroyed, along with our chance of selling it."

"Come on. Just once. I'm begging you."

"No. The answer is no. It's not insured. And it's worth too much money."

I put the key back into my pocket. Dad and I drove his old Honda over to the Peat Funeral Home on Sixth Avenue. The funeral home looked like a white mansion, nestled in among the coffee shops and restaurants. We parked right in front—few other cars were around—and walked up the gray steps to the wide wooden door.

Two men stood in the foyer: one tall and thin, the other short. They wore matching black suits and narrow black ties. The tall one hunched his shoulders and jutted his chin out like a perching crow. The short man had a bristly mustache so large it seemed to cover the bottom half of his face.

"Thank you for coming," said the tall man. He turned to his partner. "Ludwig, lead them into the chapel."

We followed the short man through a set of double doors. Rows of empty chairs filled the room. "Where is everyone?" whispered Dad.

"There is no one else," said the tall man's voice behind us. "You will be the only ones in attendance. You may sit anywhere you like."

We sat halfway back. The tall, thin man stood in the front of the room and introduced himself as Victor Peat. He thanked us again for coming. He read a brief description of Mr. Shoreby, but there was nothing I hadn't already read in the paper. Ludwig then played a short piece on an organ—it might have been "Amazing Grace," but it was played in such a gloomy style I couldn't be sure. Victor Peat then cleared his throat and addressed us again.

"The following is a letter from Mr. Shoreby himself. His will stipulated that it be read at his funeral." He began to read:

Dear attendees,
    I was planning to die many years from now. But as I write this, I know my death is imminent.
    I had a secret. You know what it was. I gave the secret away and thought I had escaped. I thought I

had gotten off scot-free. But then, just this morning, I felt a sudden urge to update my will. To pass on my favorite automobile upon my death. I put pen to paper, and it was as if an invisible force moved my hand, telling me to leave my auto to a certain Johann Silver, a man I had never met.

But Silver. I knew that name. And I know the limits of coincidence. If a Silver were to inherit my auto — if my hand was forced to write such words — then I knew I was about to die.

Dad leaned over to me and whispered in my ear, "This guy was nuts. We are definitely selling the car."

This shouldn't have surprised me. The secret always works this way. When one wins, another loses.

So let me warn you: Be rid of the thing. Sell it quickly. And protect your soul. There are more ways than one to lose it.

With great regret and great relief,
Shoreby

Victor Peat motioned for us to come forward. "It is now time to view the body." Dad pulled me to my feet.

"I am not looking at any dead guy," I whispered.

"Just do it," said Dad. "Whoever Shoreby was, he gave us a car. Just give him a quick look and we'll get out of here."

I said no again, but Dad pushed me forward. "Keep your eyes closed if you want."

I followed Victor Peat onto the platform until I was even with the black coffin. I was afraid of whom I was going to see. I was ninety-nine percent sure I knew who it would be, but I still hoped I'd be wrong.

I muttered, "I don't want to look. I don't want to look." "Shhh," said Dad.

The bottom half of the coffin was closed. I walked along it, staring down, getting ready to shut my eyes before the body came into sight. But curiosity took hold. I had to see.

I recognized the dead man instantly, just as I had feared. Shoreby was the old man from the cheese store. His thin white hair was combed neatly against his head. His face looked relaxed, as if he were deflated slightly. Heavy makeup smoothed out his wrinkles.

He wore a simple black suit. His hands were folded upon his chest. He clutched something between the fingers of his right hand. It was a single dollar bill.

Dad grabbed my elbow. "Gabe, come on."

But I couldn't stop staring at the dead man, thinking that he had rid himself of the bottle just in time to save his soul. He'd dodged the Devil, with only days to spare. And then I thought about my wish for the car—the Ferrari. I'd gotten the car. And Shoreby had gotten dead.

Dad pulled me away. "I thought you said you didn't want to look."

When Dad and I returned home, Dad stood on the sidewalk, staring at the car under the cover. He said, "I haven't found anyone to buy it yet, but I'm selling it just as soon as I can."

"So it's going?" I reached out a hand toward the Ferrari.

Dad pulled my hand back. "You heard the letter. He said to sell it quickly. It's going. Don't touch it."

"I don't think he meant the car, Dad."

"What else *could* he have meant?"

I gulped and said nothing. I went to my room and fell onto my bed. I had to turn to my side to keep from staring at the Ferrari poster. I was so lonely I texted Henry.

I got rid of the bottle. And I just came back from the funeral of the guy at the cheese store. You want to come over?

After half a minute, Henry texted back,

Let me ask my mom.

Henry knocked on the apartment door about fifteen minutes later. I gave him a quick tour, ending in my room.

"Did you see the car?" I asked.

"What car?"

I pointed out my half window to the covered car. "You'll never believe what it is. A Ferrari 430."

Henry gulped. "You wished for it?"

I nodded. "But Dad is selling it. It'll probably be gone in a day or so."

"Are you kidding? Parents are crazy. What else did you wish for?"

"My dad to get his job back. He got a call the same day."

"No more Hasty's Pizza? Dang. What else?"

I thought about my wish for a new friend, but couldn't bring myself to tell Henry. "Fifty thousand dollars. Someone to fix the hole in our living room ceiling. Oh—and one other thing."

"What?"

"It's kind of stupid."

"Tell me."

"A hot tub."

"A hot tub? A hot tub is not stupid. A hot tub is awesome. Did you get it? Where is it?"

"Nothing yet."

"Huh. But when you wished for a job, your dad got one. You wished for a Ferrari and you got one. You wished for a dollar and you got one. It seems like it really works. Where's the bottle now? You said you got rid of it."

"I loaned it to a guy upstairs."

"You what? You shouldn't let that thing out of your sight."

I slugged Henry in the arm. "Are you kidding me? You're the one who threw it off the bridge."

"I know! Because it's so creepy. But look—" Henry stared out the window at the covered car. "You got a *Ferrari*. I wouldn't mind a Ferrari. Or a Lamborghini. Or—or even a bag of candy or something."

I was about to slug Henry again when someone knocked on our front door. I opened it.

"Take it!" said Doctor Mandrake. He thrust the little bottle toward me. "Take it back. Just having it in my rooms—I feel—Oh! I feel like I have aged a millennium." He dropped his voice and leaned toward me. His breath smelled like pipe tobacco and peppermint. He placed the bottle in my hand and closed my fingers around it. "I am conflicted, young Sea Goat. I feel the need to return it to you, but I fear that I am bestowing a curse on you at the same time. It is *evil*. Look here."

Mandrake pulled a sheet of paper from inside his robe. He unfolded it. It was covered in Egyptian hieroglyphics. Mandrake ran a finger down a row until he came to an image of a bird, but with the head of a man. "See this? This is the first symbol on the bottom of the bottle. This one is easy. It means *soul*."

Mandrake ran his finger down to the bottom of the page. "Now look here. See all these little images of men? This one with the hands up means *to ask*. This one with the hands hanging down means *tired*. But this one—where the man's hands are bound behind his back—this one matches the second mark on the bottle."

I shivered. "What's that one mean?"

"It means *enemy*. Put the two marks together, young Sea Goat."

"*Soul enemy,*" whispered Henry. "That doesn't sound good."

Mandrake nodded his head. "Be done with it. Today, if possible."

A BET WITH JOANNA

"Geez," said Henry, his eyes wide. "Maybe you *should* get rid of that thing." He reached out as if to touch it, then pulled his hand back. "But before you do, let's get some lunch."

"Lunch?"

"Yeah, man. Wish for an awesome lunch. Like a ten-foot sub sandwich or a triple-pepperoni pizza."

"Did you hear a single word that Mandrake just said?"

"Oh, come on. You just told me you wished for a hot tub."

"That was before I went to the funeral. And before—all of that."

"Okay. Sure. So don't wish for such big stuff. If we—I mean you—if you just do little wishes, how can it hurt anyone? I mean, say you wish for a pizza and someone somewhere loses a pizza because of it. It's not that big of a deal to lose a pizza. You just pay ten bucks and get another one."

I nodded. "Okay, okay. I think this is a really bad idea, but what do you want?"

"Pizza."

I said, "I kind of want the giant sub sandwich. Like a Mike's Deluxe. With ham and salami and roast beef and turkey."

"Wish for some root beer, too." Henry grinned.

I held the bottle in front of me. "I wish for a giant submarine sandwich with ham and salami and roast beef. Oh, and turkey. I wish for a double-pepperoni pizza—"

"Triple!" said Henry.

"Scratch that. *Triple*-pepperoni pizza. And I wish for some root beer, too."

"How long does it take?" said Henry.

I held out the bottle again and added, "And I wish for it to be here in time for lun—"

A crash outside interrupted us. We ran to the living room window and looked down. A blue car had smashed into a white van, right in front of the Bright House. Henry and I sprinted down the stairs.

The car and van had hit each other head on. Steam was pouring out of the van. The front corner of the blue car was crushed in.

"You were over in my lane!" yelled the driver of the van.

"You were speeding," said the car driver. "You must have been going at least forty."

"Now what am I gonna do?" said the driver of the van. "I'm never going to make my delivery."

Henry nudged me. The sign on the side of the white van said MSM DELI. Everyone in Tacoma knew MSM. They made the best submarine sandwiches on the planet. The driver of the van said, "I got a giant Mike's Deluxe in the back. I got to get it out of there before the mayo goes bad."

Henry nudged me again and nodded toward the car. On the roof was a lit sign for Hasty's Pizza. I turned to the driver of the van and said, "We'll take your sandwich—I mean, if that would help."

"Take my pizza, too," said the car driver. "The smell of all that pepperoni is giving me a splitting headache. Oh, and you might as well take the root beer."

A shudder went through me as we carried all the food

back inside. The sandwich was so big it barely fit on our table. The pizza was so loaded with pepperoni that you couldn't even see the cheese beneath it. We ate. It was delicious.

Henry and I crawled into my room and sprawled on my mattress. Henry burped.

"Your burp smells like pepperoni," I said.

"Tastes even better than it smells," said Henry.

I said, "But you saw what happened, didn't you?"

"Yeah . . ." Henry's voice trailed off. "But that pizza was awesome."

"I can't believe you," I said. "You were all, 'That thing is evil,' and 'You shouldn't mess with it,' and 'I'm gonna throw it off this bridge to protect you,' and now you're just, 'That pizza was awesome.'"

"It *was* awesome."

"Yeah, and two guys almost got killed."

"They didn't almost get *killed*. They just smashed their cars. And they probably both have insurance. No one died."

"Don't you feel even a little guilty?"

"Yeah, I do. I feel guilty. But mostly, I feel full. I wish I could take a nap."

"Stop with the wishing," I said.

"Sure. We should probably stop."

"Good. Then we agree."

"Right." Henry rubbed his swollen belly. "But the possibilities! Think of what we could ask for."

"I do. I have been thinking about it. But now, every time I think about it, I also think about poor Mr. Shoreby."

"Who the heck is Mr. Shoreby?"

"He's the guy. From the cheese store."

"That guy? You call that guy *poor*? He drove a Ferrari, for goodness' sake."

"Duh. That's his Ferrari on the street, under the car cover. And Shoreby is dead."

Henry turned pale. "Dead? Like *died* dead?"

"Like I wished for a Ferrari, then Shoreby died and left Dad his car in his will. I told you I went to his funeral today."

"You killed him."

"Don't say that. Please don't say that."

"You made a wish. And now he's dead. You pretty much killed him."

"Well, you pretty much made those poor guys crash their cars."

"Me?" said Henry. "You're the one who wished."

"Yeah, because you begged me to."

Henry rubbed his stomach again. "You should get rid of that bottle. But we should have wished for some dessert, too."

Mom knocked on the door of my room. She had a football-shaped package of the leftover pizza and submarine sandwich, wrapped in aluminum foil. She told me to take it to Mrs. Sedley and Joanna.

Henry begged to come along. "If she decides to punch you in the face, I want to be there to see it."

"I'm gonna wish for your lips to be sewn together," I said.

I knocked on Joanna's door. She opened it and stared at us, then glanced down at the package in my hand.

"What's that?"

"Food. My mom asked me to bring it up."

"We don't need your leftovers. What'd you do, poison it?"

"Who's there?" said a voice from inside the apartment. "Is that the boy from downstairs? Invite him in, JoJo."

"Yeah," I said, "Invite us in, JoJo."

Joanna clenched her teeth as we stepped inside her apartment.

"Whoa," said Henry. "It's really—scarfy in here."

"What's that supposed to mean?" said Joanna.

"You know—there are lots of scarves everywhere." Scarves were draped over the backs of chairs. Scarves covered the lamp shades. Big silk scarves the color of jewels hung around the windows like curtains. Scarves even hung from the smoke detectors on the walls. It gave the room a messy, cozy feel. "I like it," said Henry, "but you gotta admit. It is super scarfy."

Mrs. Sedley's voice called from a back room. Joanna growled as she led us through a bedroom door. Mrs. Sedley lay on a bed. Her head was wrapped in another of the scarves. She looked like a tired lady pirate. I guessed she must have been bald underneath, from her sickness. She smiled. "Thanks so much for bringing lunch. I don't have much of an appetite these days, but I'm sure Joanna would love some. Wouldn't you, JoJo?"

Joanna growled again.

"Honey, introduce me to your friends. Let's see. It's Gabe, right?"

I nodded. "And this is Henry."

"It's so nice to see some kids JoJo's age in our apartment. You guys want to stay and watch a movie or something? We also have a whole closet of board games that hardly ever get touched."

"I like games," said Henry. I tried to step on his foot, but he slipped it out of the way. "You got Monopoly?"

"We sure do," said Mrs. Sedley. "Honey, go get Monopoly and bring it into the living room. I think there's some cookies on top of the fridge."

"Mom—"

"Don't argue. You need to socialize with actual humans once every few months. Just do it."

I glared at Henry on our way out. He grinned back at me.

Joanna yanked a game out of the living room closet. "I'm gonna kill both of you. First I'm gonna kill you in Monopoly. Then I'm gonna kill you in real life."

"You really need to relax," said Henry. "You could probably be nice if you just chilled out a little. Besides, Gabe is totally gonna win the game. Aren't you, Gabe?"

"What?" I said. "What are you talking about?"

"Yeah, what are you talking about?" said Joanna. "I always win. I'm ruthless."

"I bet you are, but you're not gonna win today. Gabe can win whenever he, ummm, wishes. Can't you, Gabe?"

"Not a chance," said Joanna as she opened the board and began passing out money.

"How about we make a bet?" said Henry.

"Henry, would you just shut your mouth?" I said. "I'm not gonna do it."

"Do what?" asked Joanna.

"Nothing. Doesn't matter. Because I'm not gonna do it."

Joanna said, "Fine. Then shut up about it and give me the race car."

"No, no, no," I said. "I'm *always* the race car."

"Not today," said Joanna. "You can be the top hat."

"No. You don't understand. I love cars. I am the race car. I can even tell you what kind of car it is."

"Wait. What? Are you kidding me?"

"Nineteen-forties Kurtis Kraft midget racer."

"Okay, so you're a car nerd. Who cares? I'm still the

car." She grabbed the car from Henry's hand and tossed the top hat to me.

I'd never played Monopoly without being the car. Joanna probably couldn't tell a Ferrari 430 from a Ford Model T. I turned to Henry. He was staring at me, nodding. I nodded back.

"Okay," I said. "You be the car if you want to, but you're gonna lose."

"Yeah, right."

"So how about that bet?" said Henry. "If Gabe wins, then you have to stop bullying him at school."

"Bullying him? You think I'm bullying him?"

"Yes I do. And if he wins, you have to stop. And you have to be nice to him. Really nice. Like every time you see him, you have to ask him how his day is going."

"Good lord. And what happens when I win? Do I get to kill him? Because I will win."

"Okay, Joanna, *if* you win, then, ummm, then Gabe—"

"Then Gabe and you have to be my personal butlers for a month. And you have to wear top hats—like that one."

"Done!" said Henry.

"You should have just let me be the car," I said.

"Too late," said Joanna. She rolled the dice. "Eleven. I go first. Unless one of you gets double sixes."

Gabe stared at me, then nodded toward my pocket. I reached a hand in and touched the little bottle in there. I muttered quietly under my breath. "I wish that I would win this Monopoly game I'm playing right now," I said.

"You what?" said Joanna. "You wish? You can wish all you want. I'm still gonna kick your butt."

"It's Gabe's turn to roll."

I rolled. The dice landed with two sixes facing up. Joanna frowned, but said nothing. Henry rolled a four, so I went first.

With my first turn, I began the fastest, most brutal game of Monopoly that has ever been played in the history of the world. Each time I rolled the dice, I got doubles exactly twice—enough to get extra turns, but never enough to go to jail. Each time I passed Free Parking, I landed on it and collected the money in the middle of the board. Each time Joanna rolled, she landed on one of my properties. Every minute, I grew richer and Joanna grew poorer. Soon, nearly every space on the board was covered in my houses and hotels. In less than half an hour, Joanna was broke and I won.

Joanna glared at me. "How did you do that?"

"Do what?"

"How did you win like that?"

"I don't know. I just won."

"He's lucky, I tell ya!" said Henry. "Hey, JoJo, you want to practice your part of the deal right now?"

Joanna glared at Henry. She balled up her fists. "I have to be nice to *him*. But I didn't agree to anything about you."

INSIDE HASHIMOTO'S STUDIO

WE SAT DOWN FOR DINNER that night without Dad. Mom said he was meeting with a former coworker. I shrugged and shoveled a mouthful of potatoes into my face.

Dad came home a few minutes before my bedtime, looking tired. I sat on the couch watching TV while he and Mom sat at the kitchen table, but since our apartment was so small, I could hear almost every word of their conversation. They talked about some woman named Professor Everton, whom Dad must have met with that evening. This Everton person was apparently really upset about something. Dad talked about how smart she was and how she was a world-famous sociologist. I was almost asleep when I heard him say, "It's weird to be the guy who got her job."

That line grabbed me. I moved to the end of the couch and leaned in Dad's direction so I could listen.

Mom said, "It's not your fault. And you need that job."

"I do. Sure. But she needs it, too. She's got two kids and all the bills that come with them."

"Then she must have done something."

Dad said. "Maybe so, but she says she didn't. She says she's never had a complaint more serious than a kid whining about grades. And then one day she walks into work and is just flat-out fired."

I didn't want to hear any more. I didn't need to. I knew why Everton had lost her job. I had wished to the imp for a job for Dad. And the imp had delivered. He'd taken the job away from Everton and given it to Dad. Because of me.

I started forming a speech—a confession. I practiced the words in my mind.

> *Mom, Dad. I'm the one who got Everton fired.*
>
> *Oh, really? How'd you do that, Gabe?*
>
> *I wished it.*
>
> *Oh, honey, that doesn't make it your fault.*
>
> *Yes, it does. I have this bottle. I got it from an old man at the cheese store. I wished for Dad to have a job and he got one. I wished for a Ferrari and we got one. I wished for a pepperoni pizza and I got one.*
>
> *That's nice, dear. Now you just sit down on the couch and get it together, because what you're saying is completely bonkers.*

I did feel a little unhinged. Such things don't happen in the real world. But there were Mom and Dad, still talking about how miserable Everton was—how bro-

ken she seemed. So instead of confessing, I wished. I reached into my pocket, touched the bottle, and said, "I wish for Professor Everton to get a new job."

There. Fixed. At least I hoped it was fixed. I decided to go for a walk to clear my muddled head.

"Where are you going?" said Dad.

"For a walk."

"But it's time for bed," said Mom.

"Just for a minute. I won't go far."

"Don't. Your father and I are going to sleep, so be sure to lock the door and turn off the lights when you come back in."

I nodded, then walked down the stairs toward the lobby, my head still spinning. Jimmy Hyde's music was playing from behind his door. I could hear Mrs. Hashimoto talking to someone—maybe herself—while she worked in her studio. "Yes! That's it. Beautiful as always."

The studio door opened. The figure in the doorway made me gasp. It was a woman wearing a red dress with huge white polka dots. On her head, she wore a wig of bright red hair. A face covered in spotless white stage makeup stared at me without smiling. "What do you want?"

"Me? I—nothing."

"You are staring at me as if you want something. Or perhaps my beauty is overwhelming you?"

"I—I'm—I don't mean to stare. Are you—are you Mrs. Hashimoto?" It was the first time I'd seen her door open, so I wasn't sure.

"I am not Mrs. anything. I am Hashimoto. That is how I am known."

"I live here, too. Upstairs. We just moved in."

She barked out a single laugh. "Ha. I don't live here. I work here. I have just stopped painting for the day. My studio." She waved her hand behind her. "Don't look! Not even for a second! No one looks inside the mind of Hashimoto!" She smiled. "You would still like to see, though? Of course you would."

"Sure."

"Sure? You don't sound very certain. I ask you if you want to step into Hashimoto's studio and you say *sure*. It is yes or no."

"Oh. Then yes."

"Of course, yes. When Hashimoto offers, yes is the only answer. One moment." She went in and shut the door behind her. I could hear rustling inside and what might have been whispers. I heard a door open and close. A moment later, Hashimoto stepped out. "Enter," she commanded.

I walked inside. Huge wooden panels leaned against a wall. A long workbench was covered in old coffee cans holding various brushes. Tubes of paint were organized on shelves. Rolls of white canvas stood in a corner.

Easels were scattered around the space, each holding a large canvas. Other canvases hung from three of the walls. Some were only a few feet across, while others must have been five feet wide and seven or eight feet high. I couldn't see what had been painted on any of them. Every painting in the room was wrapped in bright red fabric and tied with old rope, so that each looked like a flat, red present. And, of course, smoke detectors were hung every few feet on every wall.

"What do you think?"

"It's cool, I guess."

"You guess? Do you know how few people have been inside Hashimoto's studio?"

"Then why'd you let me in?"

"You needed to come in. You needed a distraction. I needed one, too. How do you like my work, darling?"

"I can't really tell. It's all covered up."

"What do you mean?"

"You know. It's all wrapped up—in red cloth and rope and stuff."

She frowned at me, then smiled. "You don't know Hashimoto, do you?"

"Well, no. I mean. I've just met you, so . . ."

"I mean you don't know my work! You've never seen any Hashimoto—not in galleries or museums or even in magazines or on television."

"I don't think I have."

"You haven't! You would know. This is my work. What you see in front of you! This cloth! These ropes! What they hide beneath is never to be revealed! No one is allowed to unwrap it. Ever! No one ever sees inside but me!"

"Why?"

"Exactly! That is what I want. That question. I want people to look at it and ask, *Why*? If I can get a person—you—if I can get you to ask why, well, what more on this earth could I do? Who has done greater? Tell me. Who?"

I thought for a few seconds, then nodded. "Yeah. That's pretty cool, I guess."

"No guessing. It *is* cool! It is the coolest! I am Hashimoto, the modern Alice in Wonderland! Now, forget what you have seen here and walk me to my car."

"Hey, just a sec. Can you tell me which one you're doing right now? I mean, I hear you in here, working away and talking to yourself—"

"You hear Hashimoto talking to herself?"

"Yeah. Sometimes. Which one of these are you working on?"

"Just to myself?"

"Yes."

"What do you hear me say?"

"I don't know. Not much. Mostly about how you like your work. How you think it's beautiful."

She smiled. "It is beautiful. Why would I say anything different, darling?"

"So which one are you working on?"

"Why?" Hashimoto asked. She laughed, then pointed to the eight-foot-tall canvas in the center of the room. "That one."

"So you paint it and paint it, but then no one ever gets to see it?"

"Precisely."

"But what does it look like underneath?"

Hashimoto reached out a finger and stroked one of the ropes that wrapped around the painting. "Ahh, it is the most exquisite. It is the most beautiful."

"Then why don't you—"

"Or! Or perhaps—perhaps it is the most hideous. Perhaps it is the most ugly."

"Which is it?"

"I will never tell. But I will reveal that it is a painting of a woman."

"What's it called?"

"Or! Or perhaps it is not a woman. Perhaps it is a man. Do you know what I call it?"

"What?"

"*The Mother Looking Down On the Earth and Crying.* Do you know why?"

"No."

"Do you want to know why?"

"Yes."

"Exactly." She laughed again, then pushed me out. "Stay here. I must go to the bathroom. I'm cursed with the bladder of a teacup poodle." She closed the door. I waited. I swear I heard her talking again, but couldn't hear what she said. The door opened and Hashimoto stepped out wearing a pair of round, red-framed glasses on her nose. She quickly closed the door behind her and held out her hand. "To my car."

I took her hand and led her out to the sidewalk. The only cars parked outside were Mom's pool-cleaning van, Mrs. Sedley's Volkswagen Beetle, Dad's old Honda, and the covered Ferrari. She pointed to the covered Ferrari. "I like this one," she said.

"Do you know what's under that?" I said.

Hashimoto shook her head no.

"Do you want to know?"

"Ha!" barked Hashimoto. "I like you, darling! Kisses! Kisses!" A red Lincoln Town Car pulled up right then. She gave my hand a squeeze and stepped inside.

JOANNA MAKES A BOLD REQUEST

I TRIED TO REMEMBER WHY I'D COME OUTSIDE. Hashimoto had succeeded in distracting me from what I'd done, but it all came back to me now in a rush.

I'd made Everton lose her job. I'd made Mr. Shoreby die. I'd made those two drivers crash their cars. I'd even made Joanna lose at Monopoly so I could win. The mental list of consequences weighed on me almost as much as the bottle in my pocket. I felt tired. I pulled the bottle out and stared at it.

"What are you looking at?" said a voice.

I spun around. Joanna was sitting on the steps, off in the shadows. I hadn't seen her when I first came out. I quickly slipped the bottle back into my pocket. "You have to be nice to me," I said.

"This *is* me being nice to you," Joanna said. "If you want more than this, you're gonna have to beat me at something bigger than Monopoly."

I took a step toward her, the way you might take a step

toward a bear inside a rickety cage. "What are you doing out here?"

"Just getting outside. Sometimes I need a break from my mom. She can totally drive me crazy."

"That's not a very nice way to talk about a—"

"A what? A sick person? A cancer patient? Just because she's sick doesn't make her any less annoying." Joanna laughed. "Sometimes it makes her more annoying. She's all into this positivity junk. *'We have to stay positive, JoJo. I need you to smile!'*"

"JoJo. So she calls you that all the time, huh?"

"Yeah, and if *you* call me that one *more* time, all bets are off. I will punch you so hard you'll be picking up your teeth from here to the morgue."

"You are the angriest person I've ever met," I said.

"Shut up."

"How long have you lived here?"

"Six months longer than you. The nut on the top floor has been here practically forever."

"Doctor Mandrake?"

"Yeah, but if he's a doctor, then I'm your fairy godmother," said Joanna. "The Brackleys moved in a month before you, so about six weeks ago."

"What do you think about them?" I said.

"I think they're ridiculous, but entertaining. It's like having the Kardashians for neighbors. They'll probably be gone soon. And you're probably already planning to move out."

"We've talked about it. But we're stuck here. My dad signed a one-year lease."

Joanna shook her head. "Wow. I bet he's the only one in the history of the Bright House to ever do that."

"Yeah, my dad's never been the greatest negotiator."

"Sucks for you." She rolled her eyes as a strain of Hawaiian music reached our ears. "Then you got Jimmy Hyde, who's been here exactly five years and one month."

"What's his deal?"

"No idea. You've probably noticed he barely comes out of his apartment. And you got Hashimoto, also exactly five years and one month. But she doesn't live here, so she doesn't count. And then Alejandro Aguilar, but he works here. Which brings us to his boss, good old Mrs. Appleyard, who owns the dump."

"How long has she owned it?" I said.

"I don't know. But one time when I was in Hashimoto's studio, she said Mrs. Appleyard inherited it from her husband. She says we should be happy he's gone. Apparently, he was even more of a crook than she is."

I tried to imagine someone more crooked than Mrs. Appleyard. Then I said, "So why are you living here?"

"Why do you think? Because of Mom. Turns out cancer is expensive. And she hasn't been able to work in a while. That's why I had to leave my old school and come to yours."

We were both quiet, then I said, "You just said you've been in Hashimoto's studio? She told me she never lets anyone in."

"Funny. She told me the same thing right before she gave me a tour. She's pretty weird. This whole place is weird. You can sit down if you want."

I sat on the steps a few feet away from her. She still made me nervous. She said, "So what have you got in your pocket?"

"What? Nothing."

"Come on. I know you've got something on you. You were looking at it when I came out. And you were fiddling with something in your pocket before you destroyed me at Monopoly. Let me see it."

"It's just a bottle. An ordinary bottle." I took a deep breath and pulled the bottle from my jeans and held it out. "See?"

The problem was, the bottle didn't look ordinary. It looked as if something was moving inside.

"This your good luck charm?" said Joanna. "Can I hold it?"

I let Joanna take it from my hand. She turned it slowly in the porch light. "What's in it?"

"I don't know. Probably nothing. The stopper thingy doesn't come out."

Joanna pulled at it.

"Don't!" I said, louder than I'd planned.

Joanna smiled at me. "Why? I thought you said it doesn't come out."

"Yeah, but I don't want you breaking it or anything. It's fragile. And it's really old."

"Calm down. I won't break it. Where'd you get it?"

"I—I got it—I mean—Doctor Mandrake found it out here. He gave it to me." I figured this wasn't a lie, even if it wasn't the complete truth. "Mandrake said the universe told him I should have it."

"Sounds just like something Mandrake would say. If it's so old, why do you carry it around in your pocket?"

"I don't know. I just like it, I guess."

"You *just like it*? Then here, take it." Joanna tossed the bottle up into the air. I grabbed for it, but missed. It landed on the concrete step, then bounced down, step by step, to the sidewalk below. I rushed down to pick it up.

"How is it?" said Joanna.

"Fine, I guess."

"Looks like it's not fragile. So what's the deal with the car?" She nodded toward the covered Ferrari.

"Dad's selling it."

"But it's something special, right? You seemed pretty upset about it earlier."

"It's a Ferrari 430." I told her that Dad was selling it because he wanted the money more than he wanted the car. I told her that I'd never even ridden in it.

"You're gonna sell it without even driving it once?"

"Not me. My dad."

Joanna stared at the car. "My mom is asleep. What are your parents doing?"

"Same."

"Very interesting. So, uh, where does your dad keep the key?"

I swallowed. I knew exactly what Joanna was suggesting, and it made me feel a little queasy, half from fear and half from excitement.

I had to think about where the key was right then. It took me a solid ten seconds to realize it was in my pocket. I'd had it with me since before the funeral. I pulled it out.

"You keep the most interesting things in your pockets, Gabriel Silver." Joanna walked over to the car and began pulling off the cover. "So you gonna take us for a ride or what?"

WE RIDE THROUGH THE NIGHT

I HAD A BOTTLE IN MY POCKET that I could wish on and get anything I wanted, but I don't think I've ever been as excited, as nervous, or as mystified as I was when I stood there, looking at that car with the key in my hand.

I walked over to the Ferrari and ran my hand along its shiny red roof. I felt like laughing, crying, and throwing up, all at the same time. I walked around to Joanna's side and unlocked her door, then did the same to mine. We climbed in and sat down.

"Turn it on," she said.

I took a deep breath. I slowly slipped the key into the ignition, as if it were made of glass and would break if I pushed too hard.

"Turn it on already, would you?"

I turned the key. The car made a loud whirring noise, jerked forward, and stopped. "Oops," I said. "Forgot to take it out of gear." I pushed down the clutch pedal and turned the key again. The engine roared to life. "Oh, dear God in heaven," I said. "That is the most beautiful sound I've ever heard."

"Yeah yeah yeah. It sounds great. Let's go. You know how to drive?"

"You're only asking me this now?"

She shrugged and put on her seat belt.

"I sort of know how," I said, doing the same. "My dad's let me drive on dirt roads a few times. But I've never done it on regular roads. And never in a car like this."

"No time like the present," said Joanna. "Stick the thingymajig in gear or whatever and let's get out of here."

"If I wreck this thing—if I even scratch it—my dad is gonna kill me."

"So don't wreck it," said Joanna.

"Here goes nothing," I said. I let out the clutch and the Ferrari lurched forward. I gave it a bit more gas. It jerked ahead so fast I had to slam on the brakes to keep from hitting the next car parked on the street—Dad's old Honda. The Ferrari died. I laughed nervously, started it again, and eased it into the middle of the road in first gear. I gave it just a little bit of gas, shifted into second, and we were off.

We still jerked around every now and then, and the gears made an awful grinding noise almost every time I shifted, but I got the hang of the Ferrari well enough to make it out of our neighborhood. "Where should we go?" I said.

"Let's go downtown," said Joanna. "Let's go find some life. But first, you should turn on your headlights."

I found the knob for the lights without crashing. Joanna

fiddled with the radio until she found a song she liked. Not my style of music, but I liked listening to her sing along with it.

I could get used to this, driving around in an amazing car with—well, with a girl. Maybe the bottle was worth having around after all.

I cruised along Pacific Avenue. The people out on the sidewalks—grown-ups stepping out of bars and restaurants—all seemed to stare at us as we drove by. I hoped they were looking at the car. I hoped they weren't noticing that a kid was driving.

Then I saw a red Lincoln Town Car parked outside a brightly lit glass building. "I know that car," I said. "That's Hashimoto's."

"What? Really? Let's stop."

I pulled the Ferrari over to the side of the road. It took me about three minutes to get it into a parking spot without hitting one of the cars next to it. We got out and walked up to the building.

It was an art gallery, full of people in fancy clothes. On the walls inside hung paintings wrapped in red cloth.

"Let's go in," said Joanna.

"Are you kidding? They'll kick us out. Look how those people are dressed."

"So they kick us out. That's not the end of the world. Let's go in."

Dear Reader, have you ever had a moment in life where you felt like nothing much happened, but still everything changed? Like maybe you did something simple, like take a piece of toast from the toaster, and suddenly you understood the meaning of the universe? That, Dear Reader, is called an epiphany.

When Joanna said those words, I had one—an epiphany. Joanna didn't think she was saying anything important. For her, it was just a handful of words. But for me, it was like I just learned the biggest lesson of my life. I could sit in the car. Or I could go inside. And if we got kicked out, so what? We wouldn't go to jail. No babies would die.

It was so simple. But it seemed so important. I stared at Joanna like she was some kind of genius.

"What?" she said.

"You're pretty cool."

"Awww. How sweet. Now shut up and let's go."

We went in.

I felt really young and slobby in that room. Everyone else was a grown-up. Joanna actually fit in, because she looked older than me. And her goth clothes—black dress, black tights, dyed black hair—weren't all that different from what some of the grown-ups wore.

She dragged me over to the nearest painting. "Just stare at it like you're interested."

"Okay, but there's not much to look at, unless you really like the color red."

"I do like it," she said.

"You like red? Then how come you only dress in black?"

"I like the way I look in black, but I still like red. It's . . ."

"It's what?"

"I think it's the color my soul would be, if I could see it."

"Souls have colors? And you think yours is red?"

"I think it is. Stop looking at me like that."

"I'm not looking at you. I'm looking at this price tag." I pointed to a little white card, which hung next to the painting. It read: "*Small Child Swinging the Earth on the End of a String*, oil on canvas and mixed media, Hashimoto."

Under that was the price: $30,000.

Next to that price was a tiny red sticker. The sticker said SOLD.

"Thirty thousand dollars? For a painting?" I said.

"And somebody already bought it. Wow. No wonder Hashimoto doesn't live in our building."

"Don't hate me because I am successful, darlings." We turned around. Hashimoto was standing right behind us, her arms spread wide. "Kisses, kisses. Thank you so much for coming. Your clothes are horrible, of course—especially yours, Silver—but I love that you are here. You see now that Hashimoto is known outside of your building. Known and loved. But I want to become more famous, even more famous! Come walk with me. What would you like? A glass of champagne, perhaps?"

"Umm, we're probably a little young for that," I said.

"I'm afraid we're all out of warm milk. Well, then, let's look at my work. I will show you my favorites." She marched us through the crowd, excusing herself with a refrain of "kisses, kisses" as she pushed her way through. She led us to a tiny little painting—just a few inches across—wrapped in the same red cloth, but tied with string instead of rope. "This one is the smallest work I have ever done. Just look at it. You could hang it above the sofa of a Chihuahua and it would still be too small."

The little white sign next to it listed its title as *The Dolphin of Maximum Happiness Climbs the Stairs to Heaven* and its price as $24,000. It was sold, too.

Hashimoto dragged us back across the room again until we stood in front of a single covered painting that filled an entire wall. "This is *not* the largest I have done, but it is the largest this year. I call it *Two Peaches Rise Above the Clouds While Discussing the Creation of the Universe*. Do you like it? Of course you do. Now then, if you look right over there, you will see a table just loaded with smelly cheeses and tiny fish eggs. Go and help yourselves, darlings. And thank you again for coming to my little show."

The biggest painting was sold, too. The price tag was $110,000.

Once Hashimoto had welcomed us, no one else seemed to mind that we were there. We walked along the food table, but all I could find to eat that didn't scare me were the crackers. I ate crackers until Joanna pulled me toward the door.

When we were back in the car, Joanna said, "Do you know any long, straight roads?"

"I'm afraid to ask why."

"Because this is your one and only shot with this car. I think we should go, you know, fast. This car goes fast, doesn't it?"

Dear Reader, I should have said no. I should have chugged home, parked, and put the cover back on the car. But Joanna's daring pushed me forward, right past any point of common sense. I turned north on Pacific Avenue and followed it all the way down to the waterfront, where the road went straight for miles, without any stoplights.

"This looks as good a place as any," I said. My heart began beating faster and faster.

"Then punch it," said Joanna. "Put the pedal to the metal or whatever."

I took a deep breath. "Just give me a second."

"Second's up," said Joanna. "Step on it."

I stepped on it. I pushed my foot all the way to the floor.

The car bucked forward, throwing Joanna and me back in our seats.

"Hooooly coooow," I said, through clenched teeth. I glanced down at the speedometer. We were already doing seventy miles an hour. I shifted into the next gear and hit the gas again. The speedometer climbed higher. Seventy-five, eighty, eighty-five.

"I think you should slow down now," said Joanna. My eyes flicked over to her. She was holding the armrest so tightly, it looked like she was trying to crush it between her fingers. I smiled. Joanna, the tough girl, was scared. I pushed the gas pedal all the way down. The speed kept climbing. Ninety. Ninety-five.

"Slow down!" shouted Joanna.

"Almost there," I said. The buildings and streetlights whizzed by in a blur. Just as the speedometer crept past one hundred, the yellow car pulled out.

Dear Reader, everything in my field of vision seemed to flip into slow motion right then. The yellow car was less than thirty feet in front of us. The driver of the yellow car turned our way. Her eyes widened. Her mouth opened in a noiseless scream. I noticed that she had a little wooden cross hanging from her rearview mirror. The cross caught the glare of my headlights and I thought, *I'm about to smash into that woman's car. When I do, that little cross will be destroyed and the woman will die. Joanna and I will die, too.*

Somehow, I pulled one hand from the wheel and jammed it into my pocket. I touched the bottle. The roar of the engine cloaked my words as I whispered, "I wish we wouldn't crash!"

I don't know what happened next. I don't know if we swerved around the car, jumped over it, or just passed through it like a ghost. All I know is that we were on the other side of it, driving along unhurt. In my rearview mirror, I saw the yellow car, safely cruising away in the opposite direction.

I slowed the Ferrari to a stop. Joanna was still trying to crush the armrest. "How—how did you do that?"

"That was too close," I said. "I thought we were gonna—you know . . ."

"Yeah, me too! So what happened? Why didn't we—*you know*?"

"It was too close," I repeated, hoping the shaking in my voice would make Joanna stop asking.

We drove the rest of the way home in silence. I kept the speedometer under twenty-five the whole way. I thought, *I wished not to crash. Does that mean I made someone else crash, just to save myself?*

BROKEN BONES AND LOOSE LIPS

THE NEXT MORNING WAS SUNDAY. I wanted to sleep in, but Mom made me get up. My family went out to breakfast with Henry's family, at the Old Milwaukee Café on Sixth Avenue.

I was biting into a pancake when Dad said, "So you're never gonna believe what I heard last night. The college re-hired Professor Everton."

"Really?" I said, with my mouth full. "That's good."

"Yeah. It is good. But get this: they gave her Fitzsimmons's job. And they fired Fitzsimmons. I can't figure these people out."

I managed to swallow the food in my mouth, but couldn't eat another bite.

After we ate, Henry and I asked our parents if we could walk home, since the Bright House was only about a half mile from the café.

As soon as we were alone, I said, "That was me. I'm the one that got Fitzsimmons fired." I told Henry how I'd wished for Everton's new job.

"Well, okay, so you got one guy fired. But you also got Everton rehired. So some bad, but some good, too."

"No, it's just bad. No matter what I do, someone always loses."

"Funny you should say that. I've been thinking about things you could wish for that wouldn't hurt anyone else. Or, you know, not hurt anyone very much."

"You thought wishing for a pizza wouldn't hurt anyone, remember?"

"I know. But look, you won at Monopoly and it didn't really hurt anyone. No one died. No one lost their job. It just made old What's-Her-Butt lose."

"Joanna."

"Yeah. Old What's-Her-Butt."

"She's not that bad, really."

"Not that bad? Are you serious?"

"I guess I'm not sure yet. We hung out for a bit last night."

Henry leaned in and inspected my face. "And you're still alive?"

"Yup. She kept her side of the bet."

"There. See? Something good came out of that wish. So what if you just wished for stuff like that? Winning games and stuff. Winning bets. Like, say you wished to win a soccer game. Or wished for us to win all our baseball games this year. Or wait. I know. How about if you wished to win a race—a running race. You would win. The other guy would lose. And no one would get hurt. You could become like a super famous winner at stuff. You could win every race. Every game. You could go to the Olympics, I bet."

"I don't know. Something would still go wrong."

Henry said, "Or, I guess, I could win some, too. I mean, you *could* wish for me to win, too. I suppose."

"Maybe. I dunno. I need to think this through."

"There's nothing to think through. When you wish for something, you get it. But it seems like someone else loses. Sure, you feel bad when one person gets a job, and another person's fired, but in this case, you wouldn't have to feel bad, because all anyone would be losing is a race."

"Yeah, but—"

"But nothing. Let's just try it. As an experiment. Look— we can see your building from here. Let's race these last two blocks. And you can wish that you'll win."

"But I'd beat you anyway."

"Not if you give me a head start," said Henry. He took off running, right down the middle of the street. "You'd better get wishing!"

I shouldn't have given in. I should have at least thought about it a bit more. But all I could see was Henry beating me in a footrace. So I pulled the bottle from my pocket. "I wish that I beat Henry home," I said. Then I jammed the bottle back into my pocket and took off.

By the time I started, Henry was halfway there. It would take a miracle for me to catch him. I waited for the miracle to kick in—the sudden burst of speed that turned me into an Olympic runner. I strained forward, willing it to happen, longing for the transformation, hoping.

Instead, a blue car careened around the corner, almost hitting me. I wondered if somehow the imp had willed the car to hit me. No. That didn't make sense.

As the car zoomed ahead, I realized what was happening. I stopped running and watched as the car drew closer to Henry, who was sprinting across the street. I started screaming Henry's name. He turned around just as the car slammed on its brakes. The brakes squealed. Smoke rolled out from the tires. I heard a horrible thud as the car clipped Henry.

I ran toward him. The driver leapt out of his car. We both reached Henry at the same time. He was lying on the ground, clutching his arm. It bent away from his body at an unnatural angle.

"I'm so sorry!" said the driver. "I didn't see you, kid. You were in the middle of the street. What were you doing in the middle of the street?"

"I think my arm's broken," moaned Henry.

"I'm gonna get help," I said. "Stay here."

I ran the rest of the way home and yelled for help. Mrs. Appleyard strolled out of her unit, lighting a cigarette. "Where's the fire, Ten Cents?"

I stared at Mrs. Appleyard, trying to decide if I should ask her for help or just keep running upstairs. "My friend— he just—just got hit by a car," I said between breaths.

"He dead?"

"I need to call 9-1-1."

"Who's stopping you?" said Mrs. Appleyard. She pulled out a lighter and lit her cigarette.

I shook the panic from my head and pulled my cell phone out of my pocket. I gave the 9-1-1 operator my address, then ran back over to Henry. The driver was kneeling next to him. "Where'd you go?" said the driver.

I held up my phone. "I ran home to call 9-1-1."

"Why did you run home if you have a cell phone?"

Why did I? Had the bottle made me run there, just to complete the wish? Did it have that kind of power—over me?

Henry groaned. "It really hurts. This is my throwing arm, too."

"I'm just glad you're not dead," I said.

"That makes two of us." The driver stood up and started pacing.

"Did you notice who hit me?" said Henry. I looked at the driver and realized I'd seen him before. It was the pizza delivery man who'd crashed into the sub sandwich man. His blue car had the same dented fender. The Hasty's sign was still on top.

"Hey," said Henry, "since I have to lie here, ask him if he has any spare pizza."

Mrs. Sedley came down the steps of the Bright House, wearing a white bathrobe and dragging Joanna after her. "I heard the crash," said Mrs. Sedley. "Did you already call for an ambulance?"

I nodded yes. Mrs. Sedley asked what happened. I told her. She made sure I called Henry's parents and told them, too.

"I was totally winning," said Henry, "until that stupid car hit me." Then he looked at me, his eyes wide. We both knew why the car hit him.

"I said I was sorry," said the Hasty's driver. "You shouldn't have been running in the road."

"You shouldn't have been driving so fast," said Joanna. "I heard your tires squeal when you turned the corner. And look at your skid marks. You're lucky you slammed on your brakes or you probably would have killed him."

A funny surge of emotion—I'm not sure if it was guilt or relief—swept over me when Joanna said that. I felt guilty for almost killing my friend. I felt relief that he was still alive. But I felt a different kind of relief, too. Relief that Joanna was on our side.

An ambulance roared around the corner, its siren blaring. A police car followed immediately after, and the officer began questioning the driver and Mrs. Sedley. The police never asked me anything. Henry's mom and dad arrived just in time to follow the ambulance to the hospital. I told Henry I'd come and visit him. After a few more minutes, the street was empty again.

Joanna and Mrs. Sedley began walking back toward the apartment. I could see that they were talking. Mrs. Sedley was hissing words at Joanna. Joanna was shaking her head no. Finally, Joanna's shoulders slumped and she walked back to me.

"My mom wants me to ask if I can go with you."

"Go with me where?"

"To the stupid hospital. To visit your stupid friend."

"Gee. Thanks for the support. But I'll be fine on my own."

"Just shut up and say I can go, okay?" said Joanna. "My mom's gonna make me. I'm gonna end up going. So just agree now and we can be done with this."

"Fine, but remember that you're still supposed to be nice to me."

"Just tell me when you're leaving."

An hour later, Dad dropped off Joanna and me outside Tacoma General and said he'd pick us up when we were done. "I wonder where Henry is," I said, as I looked up at the huge building.

"He's gonna be across the street. That's where they take kids. Trust me. I spend a lot of time at this place."

"With your mom?"

"Yes, genius. With my mom."

"She's pretty sick, huh?"

"Can we not talk about it? Just try to keep up." I followed Joanna across J Street to another building. A sign above the doors said SHOREBY WING. I swallowed. A receptionist told us how to find Henry. When we entered his room, his arm was in a sling and a sleepy look was in his eyes. He turned toward us and smiled.

"Hey, Gabe," he said. A trickle of drool seeped from the corner of his mouth. "You came to visit me. That's—that's so sweet, Gabe. Gaby. Gaby Baby." He giggled, then noticed Joanna. "Oh. Hi, What's-Her-Butt."

"It's Joanna," I said.

Henry grinned. "It sure is. Old JoJo. I didn't know you came, too. I don't even like you. Because" —Henry wiped the drool from his face—"because you're not . . . very . . . nice!" He giggled. "Not very nice, but here you are, visiting me. I guess that's nice. Hee-hee."

Joanna rolled her eyes. "Are you on painkillers or something?"

Henry sighed. "I sure am. Muscle relaxants, too. I feel really relaxed. I mean *really relaxed*. Hey! Hey, Gaby Baby. Looks like neither of us won the race, eh, partner?

Because I didn't make it to the building, but neither did you!"

"Actually, I did make it, Henry. I ran there to get help. Remember?"

"You made it?" Henry's voice rose until it was high and squeaky. "Then you did win. That little imp in the bottle granted your wish again!"

"Say what?" said Joanna. Her eyes turned on me.

"Shut up, Henry," I said.

"Right!" slurred Henry. "I won't say another word." He drew his fingers across his mouth as if he were zipping it closed. "Zip my lips. Zip 'em up. Not another word about your magic bottle. Not . . . another . . . word!" He rolled his head around until it was looking toward Joanna. "Hey, JoJo."

"Hey, Henry."

"You think you're tough. But you're actually kind of cute. You've got nice lips. Zip your lips." Henry's eyes grew wide. "Did I just say that out loud, or did I just think it inside my head?"

"You said it out loud."

"That's not good. JoJo, pretend I didn't say that. About how nice your lips are. Zip 'em. Zip your nice lips. Okay?"

"Okay, Henry."

Henry frowned. "Hey, JoJo. Did you know that Gabe cheated when he beat you at Monopoly?"

Joanna punched me. "I knew it! I knew you cheated."

"Shut up, Henry," I said.

"Oh. Right. Shut up. Zippity doo-dah. But he totally cheated. He's got a magic bottle and he wished to beat you."

"What?"

"Magic. Wish for a car. Poof! You got a car. Wish for a pizza. Poof. Pizza. Hey, Gaby Baby. Remember that pizza? That was awesome. I could totally go for a pizza right now. Quad—quad—quadruple pepperonizzzzz . . ." Henry closed his eyes and started to snore.

THE BOTTLE DRAWS BLOOD

WHEN JOANNA AND I MADE IT HOME from the hospital, she demanded that I tell her everything. I gave in. I confessed how I'd gotten the bottle imp from Shoreby. I told her everything I'd wished for and I explained how every time a wish came true, something bad seemed to happen to someone else. I even told her that the one wish I'd made—for a new friend—was the only wish that hadn't come true, because Lancaster had turned out to be a dud. She laughed. "Yeah, one time my mom made me take a plate of cookies over to Lancaster's family. I argued that they could buy their own cookies, but she made me take them anyway. Guess what he said when I dropped them off."

"That he could buy his own cookies?"

"Exactly. But seriously, you don't really believe this bottle did all this, do you?"

"I do."

Joanna shook her head. "It's just coincidence. You met

a guy and then a few days later, he left a car to your dad. It seems amazing, because the two things happened close together, but that's why they call it a coincidence. Because it *seems* amazing."

"Then how did I beat you at Monopoly? You said yourself you never lose."

"Another coincidence. I happened to be unlucky on the day you were lucky. You'll never beat me again."

"Then why didn't we die?"

"Die?"

"Yes! In a car accident in the Ferrari."

"I don't—"

"You want to know why? Because I wished we wouldn't. I wished we would live."

"Oh, sure. Right. You wished and we somehow magically went around that car."

"That night you asked me why we survived. Now I'm telling you!"

"Come on, Gabe, there are close calls in cars every day. You think they're all because of magic?"

We argued back and forth about it for a while until Joanna asked to see the bottle.

"You've seen it already. You've even held it. Remember? Right before we went for a drive, when we were sitting on the steps?"

"*That* bottle?"

"Of course, *that* bottle," I said, handing it over to her. "You think I have more than one?"

When she held it, she said, "It *is* pretty creepy. I didn't really notice that before. It has a funny feel to it. But you can't really believe there's some little creature in here. A—what did you call him again?"

"An imp."

"Which is what exactly?"

"Shoreby said it was like a tiny little devil. A djinn, he called it."

"Convenient that the top doesn't come off. That way, you can never be proven wrong." She shook the bottle. "Hold on, little imp! It's an earthquake!"

"Stop it!" I said. "You don't know what you're messing with."

Joanna laughed and tossed the bottle back to me.

I called Henry's house that night. His mom said he was home from the hospital, but too miserable to come to the phone. I guess the painkillers finally wore off. She said I could come over the next day after school—Henry should be feeling okay by then.

The next day at lunch, I sat by myself in the cafeteria. Joanna sat by herself, too. We nodded at each other. She might have even smiled a tiny bit. But neither of us moved from our solo seats.

I saw her again in Miss Kratz's language arts class. Joanna sat in Henry's empty seat. When Miss Kratz turned her back, Joanna asked if I'd talked to Henry. I told her I was going to see him after school. She asked if she could come along.

"Your mom making you?"

"She probably will, so I might as well just go."

Miss Kratz turned around. "You two have something you want to share with the whole class? No? Then can you do like I do and at least pretend you want to be here?"

We walked to Henry's house after school. Joanna didn't mention the bottle once. Neither did I.

Henry was home alone and lying on the couch in the living room, with his arm wrapped in a hard cast. His other hand was wrapped around a bowl of potato chips. He smiled at me, then saw Joanna. "Oh, hey," he said. "My mom didn't tell me you were both coming."

Joanna blushed.

Henry said, "I mean, it's totally fine."

"How's the arm?" said Joanna.

"It's not too bad, today. They put a real cast on it this morning. You guys want to sign it?"

I took a Sharpie from the coffee table and wrote *GABE* in fat black letters. Joanna wrote *Know your own bone.*

"What's that mean?" asked Gabe.

"I don't know. It's something Hashimoto once said to me. I think it sounds cool."

"Who's Hashimoto?" said Henry.

"An artist. Works in our building. Either crazy or a genius. Probably a genius." Beneath the quote, Joanna signed her name in a tiny script—so small it was nearly impossible to read. She said, "Speaking of crazy, you were saying some pretty kooky stuff yesterday."

Henry laughed. "That's what I've heard. Mom said I kept telling her I loved everybody and kept asking what was for dinner. What kind of goofy stuff did I say to you guys?"

"You told Joanna you thought she was cute," I said.

Henry gulped. "I did what?"

"You said she had nice lips."

"Oh, man." Henry's face turned pale. "I'm really sorry."

"Then you told her about the bottle imp."

Henry looked back and forth between Joanna and me.

"Don't worry," said Joanna. "I don't believe it. Bunch of nonsense. You don't believe it, do you?"

"'Course I do," said Henry. "You would, too, if you'd been there when we—when Gabe wished for lunch. We were specific. We asked for a double-pepperoni pizza—"

"Triple," I said.

"Right. A triple-pepperoni pizza and a Mike's Deluxe and that is exactly what we got. I mean, we got it right out front. Within like thirty seconds. Exactly what we ordered."

"It still has to be a coincidence. That kind of stuff just doesn't happen."

"Well, it happened," said Henry. "And this cast even happened because of it."

"Why? Gabe wished you'd break your arm?"

"No. Gabe wished to win a race against me. I was winning until I got hit by a car."

"You think this bottle is why you got hit?"

"It *is* why," I said.

Joanna said, "I've been thinking about how convenient it is for a bottle that supposedly holds an imp in it to have a stopper you can't open. So you can't look inside it."

"You said that yesterday."

"I know what I said. But it gave me an idea. We can prove if it's real or not right now. Here, let me show you. Give me the bottle."

"What are you gonna do with it?"

"Just give it to me. It's supposed to be indestructible anyway, so what do you care?"

I pulled the bottle from my pocket. Joanna grabbed it and held it between her hands, her thumbs on each side of the bottle's neck. "Now, wish."

"Wish what?"

Joanna swallowed. "Wish to see it."

A chill wind seemed to blow through Henry's living room. Goose bumps broke out on my arms. "Wish to see what?"

"Wish to see the imp. The little devil. Whatever it is. If this thing really answers your wishes, then it will have to show itself, right? Then we'll know. If it happens, it's real. If nothing happens, then I'm right and this whole thing is a bunch of coincidences."

"There's no way I'm wishing that," I said.

"Don't do it," said Henry. "I don't want to see it. It might make us go blind or something."

"Don't worry. I'm not gonna do it."

"Do it," said Joanna.

I blew out my breath. "This is not a good idea."

"It's a great idea," said Joanna, "because you know and I know that the imp is not real. So nothing will happen. That's what you're really afraid of."

"No, that is definitely not what I'm afraid of."

"I think it is. You're afraid that you made this whole thing up in your mind."

"Joanna—"

"You're afraid to find out that there's no imp. That there's no magic."

"Will you just stop talking?"

"You're afraid that your soul is not actually in danger.

You're afraid to find out that your life is just ordinary." She frowned. "Just like everyone else."

"You are so annoying," I said. I reached out my hand and touched the bottle.

"You have to touch it?" said Joanna.

"I don't know if you have to, but I have every time. It feels like what I should do. Now shut up." I cleared my throat. "I wish for—" I stopped.

"What are you doing?" said Joanna. "Keep going."

"Look," I said. "If it is real. . . . If the old man was telling the truth and this thing really came from the Devil—"

"It's not real. Just finish the wish."

I nodded. I closed my eyes. "I wish—I wish for the imp inside the bottle to show itself. Now."

It was broad daylight when I spoke, but as soon as the words were out of my mouth, the light from the window darkened. The electric bulbs flickered and turned off, leaving us in a room of shadows. Joanna sucked in her breath. Her hands shook as she held the bottle. Henry sat forward, his eyes wide and his mouth hanging open.

The little bottle began to vibrate. It hummed. I heard a snap, as if a seal had broken. In the dim light, I could see the stopper in the top of the bottle begin to move, just barely. The movement was so slight, I wasn't sure if it had moved at all.

"Did you see that?" I said.

No one answered.

The stopper moved again. This time we all saw it. It began to turn, once around, then again, then once again.

"Holy moly," said Henry.

The stopper quit turning. The vibrating ceased, too. Nothing happened for half a minute. I let out my breath.

"What just happened?" said Joanna.

"There. You see?" I said. "You believe it now?"

"I—I don't know. It doesn't make any sense. But, I mean, I don't know. We still didn't see anything."

"Look!" said Henry.

The stopper rose slowly. It cleared the top of the bottle and kept rising, held up by two tiny claws. A tiny head rose up next, with pointy ears, bulging eyes, and a sharp

99

snout. The head twitched about, looking first at Henry, then at me, and then its gaze landed on Joanna. The creature looked down at Joanna's thumbs, holding the bottle. It hissed.

The imp jerked out, raising its gray, sinewy body halfway above the rim. It opened its mouth wide, showing rows of needle-sharp teeth. With a lurch, it clamped its teeth on the flesh of Joanna's thumb and bit down hard. Joanna let out a scream. The bottle fell to the floor.

Joanna grasped her injured thumb. Blood oozed from her wound and dripped onto Henry's coffee table.

"I believe it," said Joanna, between moans. "I do I do I do."

The bottle lay on the carpet, resting against the bottom of the couch. It was still. I nudged it with the toe of my shoe. Nothing happened. I bent down and picked it up, then quickly set it on the table and backed away.

The stopper was back in place. The bottle looked as if it had never been opened.

I MAKE A DEAL WITH LANCASTER

I WAS DONE WITH IT. I swore out loud, then and there, that I would never make a wish of the bottle imp again.

Dear Reader, it wasn't a lie. I never wished from it after that day.

When the words came out of my mouth, Henry nodded. Joanna stared at me wide-eyed, sucking on her injured thumb.

I carried the bottle back home from Henry's house in a plastic grocery bag. I couldn't bear to put that creature back into my pocket. Knowing that the imp had been there, so close to my skin, all that time, made me shiver. I could still see those bulging eyes and sharp teeth.

Joanna walked back with me, but didn't say a word. Her thumb was wrapped in a huge white bandage. When we reached the Bright House, I saw Mrs. Appleyard across the street, standing in the doorway of Hank's Bar. She was smoking a cigarette and blowing the smoke up into the afternoon. "Hey, lovebirds. Whatcha got in the bag? You two go grocery shopping together? Like an old married couple?"

She cackled. "Hey, have I ever told you about the time Mr. Appleyard did the grocery shopping?"

"*Nope,*" I shouted, and then dragged Joanna inside the Bright House. We stopped outside of my apartment. "Are you really going to get rid of it?" said Joanna.

"You don't think I should keep it after that, do you?"

Joanna said nothing.

I nodded toward the door across the hallway. "I'm sure I could sell it to Lancaster. I bet you he'd buy it in a second."

"You could sell it to me," said Joanna.

"An hour ago, you didn't even think it was real."

Joanna glared at me, then held out her bandaged thumb.

I shook my head. "I don't want any friend of mine—"

"Is that what I am?"

"What?"

"A friend of yours?"

I shrugged. "Aren't you?"

"I guess I am. But maybe it wasn't my choice. Maybe I'm the answer to your wish—you know, for a new friend."

"Maybe you are."

"If you got a friend, who do you think lost one?"

"I don't know," I said, "but if we're really friends, then I'm not gonna sell you the bottle. I don't want anything to do with it anymore. You don't know what it feels like to own it. It weighs you down."

"What if I need it more than anyone else?"

"For what?"

"You know for what. You know how much I need—something."

"Joanna, it wouldn't end well. When one person wins . . ."

"Just shut up then. I get it." I didn't see any tears, but Joanna wiped her face with the back of her hand. She nodded toward Lancaster's door. "So if you sell it to Lancaster, what do you think he'll do with it?"

"I don't know and I don't care," I said. "I just want to be done with it. I don't want it to be my responsibility anymore."

"But that's the problem, isn't it?" said Joanna. "You're the one selling it. You're the one who chooses whom you sell it to. So you're still kind of responsible, aren't you?"

"You don't think I should sell it to Lancaster? You think I should keep it?"

"I didn't say that. But, I mean, if Lancaster does bad stuff with it, aren't you partly to blame?"

"That's like saying if I sell a guy a chair and he bashes someone over the head with it, it's my fault a guy got bashed over the head."

"A chair doesn't cause car wrecks. A chair doesn't have a little devil inside it."

I stared at Joanna. "Why are you doing this? I thought you wanted me to get rid of it."

"I do. I guess."

"I can't just hold on to it. I don't think I could resist using it again. And besides, what if—what if I died when I had it? I don't want the Devil to get my soul."

"I don't want that, either. You're right. You should sell it. Sell it to whoever you can." Joanna left me standing between the two doors.

I sold it.

I coaxed Lancaster away from his Xbox and walked him outside. When I told him the story and the rules of the bottle, he acted just like you'd expect. He rolled his eyes, smirked, and asked when he could go back in. I kept talking, telling him about the car, the pizza, and the race. I didn't tell him about the imp biting Joanna's thumb. Maybe I should have.

"So get to the point, Silver. How much you want for this wondrous thing?"

"Like I said, I have to sell it for less than I bought it. So, ninety-nine cents."

"Why so cheap? What's the catch?"

"I already told you the catch. Your eternal soul. And, you know, bad stuff seems to happen. Not to you. To other people."

"Yeah yeah yeah. But what's the *real* catch? What do *you* get? I mean, I know you're poor, but ninety-nine cents ain't enough to help anyone. Even bums ask for a dollar."

"I get out."

"See! Then there is a catch. What do you get out from?"

"I get out of hurting anyone else."

"You sure are hung up on that." He dug around in his pocket. "I still get the feeling you're tricking me. That you're gonna get me some other way."

"I'm not."

Lancaster pulled out a dollar bill. "Here. You can keep the change."

"I can't. It's got to be ninety-nine cents. Not a cent more." I gave him one penny back, then reminded him that when he sold it, it had to be for less than that. Then I said the words: "Lancaster Brackley, from Tacoma, Washington, I take your ninety-nine cents in exchange for the bottle and the imp."

Lancaster grabbed the bottle from me. "I know this is a scam. I just haven't figured out how yet." He went inside and shut the door. I felt lighter. I felt safer. I breathed deep.

The Brackleys moved out of the Bright House three days later.

Lancaster's first wish was for his dad to buy a winning lottery ticket. Mr. Brackley got one worth $7.5 million dollars. I know this because Lancaster gave me a ten-dollar bill to thank me for selling him the bottle. I wondered what had happened to someone else so that the Brackleys could win that ticket. I never found out.

I saw Lancaster in the hallway, dodging an army of furniture movers. "You're crazy for selling this to me," he said. "I mean, what are you still doing in this trash heap of an apartment building when you had this? I made one wish and we're out of here."

"You getting your old house back?"

"Heck no! I wished for a new house. A mansion. The biggest one in town."

"What about the people who already live there?"

"Quit your worrying. I wished them a new house."

"Yeah, but where'd *that house* come from?"

"I don't know. Somewhere else."

"Some other person will lose their house to fulfill your wish."

"Big deal, then I'll wish a new house for them, too. A better house."

"Don't you get it? That house will have to come from somewhere, too. Somewhere, at the end of the line, you're messing up someone's life."

"Geez, Silver. You worry too much." Lancaster nudged me in the chest. "That's why you sold this to me. Because you're a worrier. Hey, I was gonna tell you something you might like. Some good news for you."

"Yeah?"

"I told my dad he should try to help you guys out—you know, financially. So he said he'd do a solid by you all."

"And?"

"He's gonna buy that car from your dad. The Corvette."

My heart sank. "It's not a Corvette. It's a Ferrari. A 430."

"Whatever. He's gonna buy it for a hundred grand. Said it can probably be my car in a couple of years, when I turn sixteen. Maybe I'll keep it. I don't know. I might wish for something nicer."

I felt my face growing hot. "There is nothing nicer."

"Yeah. Well. It's not like it's new. If I'm gonna drive a car to school, I don't want to drive a used one."

The next day, I stood on the sidewalk, watching the Ferrari pull away on the back of a truck. Lancaster and his parents were gone. Mrs. Appleyard stood behind me, blowing smoke toward the back of my head. "They was fancy people. Fancied up the joint. Didn't even want their damage deposit back. That's real class."

I couldn't help thinking about what might have been. I could have made a couple of big wishes. My family could have been billionaires. I could have flown around in a private jet. Could have had a yacht, servants, a helicopter, horses for my sisters.

But every time I thought about what I might have wished for, I also thought about whom I might have hurt.

A SERIES OF SQUEAKS

THIRTY SECONDS LATER, Mrs. Appleyard grabbed me by the arm and pulled me across the street toward Hank's Bar.

"Come with me for a sec, Ten Cents. I've got a question for you." She towed me inside and we sat down at her booth, right inside the door. She yelled at the bartender. *"One of mine, Hanky. And a Coke for this fine young man!"*

"He ain't supposed to be in here!" Hank yelled back.

"He's leaving in a sec. I promise." Mrs. Appleyard lit a cigarette, even though there was a NO SMOKING sign right by our table. She took a big drag and blew smoke up toward the tar-stained ceiling.

"Them Brackleys," she said. "It's weird them moving away all sudden like that."

"Weird how?"

"Well, I've been through the Brackley cycle three or four times already. Daddy Brackley hits it big on whatever he does with money—"

"Hedge funds is what Lancaster said."

"Sure. Whatever. Anyway, Daddy hits it big and they move out. Daddy goes broke and they move back in. But this time is different because, well, for one, they never hit it this big before. And for two, this time it wasn't Daddy."

"I don't know what you mean."

"Sure you do, because I *know* that Lancaster told you, same as he told me, a bunch of times. He said, 'This time it was me. And this time, we're gone for good. Or at least I am.' So the question is, Ten Cents, the question is, what the hell is going on?"

I took a sip of my Coke and shrugged. Mrs. Appleyard sipped her red fizzy drink without taking her eyes off me. She smiled. "I know you're part of it, because ever since you moved in, you've been sneaking around as if you're hiding something. I know sneaking, Ten Cents. Mr. Appleyard, bless him, invented sneaking. I married sneaking, till death did us part. And your dad—your *daddy*—got his job back and got that fancy car and, well, this ain't the kind of place where that stuff happens. People who live at the Bright House don't inherit Ferraris."

I shrugged again. "I should probably go. Hank said I'm not supposed to be in here."

Mrs. Appleyard squashed out her cigarette, right on the tabletop. Her side of the table was covered in black scars—burn marks from cigarettes. She said, "Mr. Appleyard, if he was here, he wouldn't let you leave until you confessed everything. He wasn't nice like me. Lord, I loved that man. Had discipline. Did you know that Bright House was our fourth apartment building?"

"You own other ones?"

"Not own. *Owned.* They're gone now. Each one burnt down. Weirdest string of coincidences, Ten Cents. Like they was on a schedule—every eight years."

I gulped. "When was the last one?"

"The last fire? Let me see . . . seven years and . . . and boy, time really sneaks up on you, don't it? But as I was saying, Mr. Appleyard could keep to a schedule."

"Why would he burn down his own apartment buildings?"

"Ten Cents, why would you say such a thing? To accuse my dear, late husband of such dreadful destruction. The man *was* a genius when it came to insurance policies, I'll grant you, but to accuse him of burning buildings? It won't stand. I won't let it." She pulled out another cigarette and tapped it on the table. "Mr. Appleyard died four years ago. Sad he didn't get to see this one through, too. Now me, I don't care as much about insurance and such things. Sure, I could use the money. But it's the memory of the man that motivates *me*. The memory of Mr. Appleyard. 'The schedule is everything,' he used to say. And if the schedule was everything for him, then it is for me, too." She lit the cigarette and puffed on it until the end was glowing hot. "'Course, I'm also a lot more considerate than he was. Softer, you might say. More motherly." She blew smoke right into my face. "So tell Mother what's going on."

"I—I don't know what you mean."

She grabbed my hands and squeezed them until it hurt. "You've got a secret and I want to know it. If you don't tell me, I'll—I'll kick your family out."

I think she saw my face brighten with hope as I said a quick prayer that she would make good on her threat.

Instead she squeezed tighter. "Let's try this again, Ten Cents. If you don't tell me—and I mean soon—then I'll move it up."

"Move what up?"

"The schedule. Keep your old secret if you want. But if you don't tell me, I'll move up the schedule."

"You're threatening me," I said. "I think that's against the law."

"I ain't threatening you, Ten Cents. I'm giving you options."

A scream from our apartment building interrupted our

conversation. It was Mom. I jerked my hands free from Mrs. Appleyard and sprinted across the street. I heard Mrs. Appleyard following me, but didn't look back. I flew up the stairs to our door. In the middle of our living room, Mom and the rest of my family were standing around a steaming, bubbling hot tub.

"But where did it come from?" asked Mom. "Hot tubs do not just appear in apartments on their own."

"It's so awesome," said Georgina.

"Soooo awesome," echoed Meg. They ran to their room, probably to change into their swimsuits.

"I don't know any more about it than you do," said Dad. He dipped a finger into the water. "It's warm. Feels nice."

"I don't care how it feels, Johann, we are not keeping a hot tub in our living room. A hot tub! In our living room!"

"I'm gonna get my suit," I said.

"You're what?" said Mom.

"I'm gonna get my suit. Then I'm gonna climb in for a soak. Because you and Dad are gonna get rid of this. Just like you did with the Ferrari. If there's something cool in our lives, you guys always get rid of it."

"Gabe—"

"So before that happens, I'm gonna at least try it out."

I marched into my bedroom. I had to dig through my drawers for a while to find my suit. I hadn't gone swimming since before we moved. I put my suit on and walked back into the living room.

They were all in it—Meg, Georgina, Dad, and even

Mom. She'd apparently gotten over her anger enough to try it out.

"Come on in, Gabe," Georgina said, blowing bubbles.

I climbed in with them.

"No splashing," said Meg.

"Yeah," said Georgina. "Mom doesn't want to get the floor wet."

"I don't suppose this means we're keeping it," I said.

"We can't," said Mom. "I'm sure if Mrs. Appleyard found out, it would be against the rules. And all the steam. It would cause mildew. I've seen what happens when people have hot tubs indoors. Not pretty."

"Besides," said Dad, "all this water is really, really heavy. I'm sure our floor isn't designed to hold this much weight. This thing is probably filled with five hundred gallons. At eight pounds a gallon, that's—whoa. That's four thousand pounds. That's a lot of pounds."

"Okay, okay. I get it. But can we at least keep it for a little while?"

Mom and Dad looked at each other. Mom sighed and nodded. Dad said, "One week. And then we need to figure out how to get it out of here. How do you think it got in?"

We sat theorizing in the warm, bubbly water. The girls thought maybe we'd won a contest. Dad thought someone might have delivered it by mistake. Mom guessed that Shoreby left it to us in another section of his will. I said maybe the hot-tub fairy paid us a visit.

I suppose I could have told them the truth—that I'd wished for it. I probably should have. But the bottle was out of my life and I didn't want to speak about it again. So I listened to them talk, then dunked my head under the warm water.

When I came above the surface, Dad shushed everyone. "Did you hear that?"

"Hear what?"

"A squeak."

We all listened, but all I could hear was the bubbling of the water.

"Must be nothing," said Dad, but then we all heard it—the squeak of groaning wood, like the sound an old nail makes when you pull it from a board.

"I heard it that time," said Mom. "What is it?"

We heard another squeak—much longer and louder this time. It was coming from right beneath us.

"It's not good," said Dad. "Four thousand pounds. Not good."

The squeak grew into a shriek, then turned into the sound of ripping and breaking. The heavy hot tub crashed through our floor, with us in it.

We all screamed. We landed with a boom in the middle of Mrs. Appleyard's apartment. The hot tub broke in two. Dad and I fell backwards out of one half of it. Mom and the girls fell out of the other half. The water burst out onto the floor of Mrs. Appleyard's apartment.

The bathroom door opened. Mrs. Appleyard stepped out, an unlit cigarette hanging from her lips. She stared at us as if we were aliens who'd just crashed a spaceship into her building. She looked down at the floor, where her bare feet were standing in four inches of water. She looked up at the ceiling, at the huge hole that gaped into our apartment. She looked at Dad.

"You are definitely not getting your damage deposit back."

THE SEA GOAT AND THE BULL

IT TOOK WEEKS TO SORT THE WHOLE MESS OUT. Mrs. Appleyard wanted to know why we had a hot tub in our apartment. Of course she didn't believe Dad when he said it just appeared there, full of hot water. She told him he was going to have to pay for the damages.

"Isn't the building insured? said Dad.

"'Course it's insured," said Mrs. Appleyard, "but insurance doesn't cover gross negligence, and bringing a hot tub into a second-story apartment is very negligent and very gross. So I'm not giving you options. You gotta pay cash money. Besides, I like to save my insurance claims for big things."

"How is this not a big thing?" said Dad.

"*Big*-big things," said Mrs. Appleyard. "Building-size things."

It cost about half the money Dad had gotten from selling the Ferrari to repair all the damage. Dad said he could have done it himself for a fourth of that. Every time he saw

Mrs. Appleyard, he said, he came away feeling that she'd cheated him out of a few more thousand in repairs.

Finally, the floor got fixed. Mrs. Appleyard ended up with all new furniture and all new carpets in her apartment. We had the same crappy rug we'd had before. And we still had that same old hole in our ceiling.

A week after the last repairman left, Joanna and I were sitting on our couch. There was a knock on the door. I opened it to Doctor Mandrake.

"Good morning, Madam. Good morning, young Sea Goat. Or is it afternoon?"

"It's two o'clock."

"And what a lovely time of day that is." Mandrake stretched his arms above his head and yawned. "For the last few weeks, I have had the most delicious sleep, night after night. I feel like a king. Or a czar. Peter the Great. Dear England's own Alfred the Great. One of the greats, to be sure."

"Okay."

Mandrake leaned in close to me and whispered. "It's gone, isn't it?"

"Isn't what?"

"The bottle. It's out of the building." He held up his hand. "Don't bother answering. I can tell."

I nodded. "Been gone for a couple of weeks."

"I knew it! I knew it! That's why I'm sleeping again. Not long after those atrocious Brackleys moved out, I nodded off on my chaise lounge. Luckily, I was already in my pajamas."

"Aren't you always in your pajamas?" asked Joanna.

Mandrake ignored her. "And then I slept! I've been sleeping twelve hours a day since then and feel as rested as Rip Van Winkle. I knew the wretched thing was gone."

Joanna said, "If you were so sure about it, why did you have to come and ask?"

"You are a skeptical one, aren't you, young lady? Well, on a day like today, even your skepticism does not bother me. Sea Goat, I would like to thank you for expunging that object from the premises. Come up to my chambers and I will give you a reading, free of charge. And perhaps a cup of Earl Grey, also free of charge."

"Can Joanna come, too?"

Mandrake frowned. "Can you keep her quiet?"

Joanna rolled her eyes. "Fine. But I'll be keeping myself quiet."

"Should we come with you now?"

"Now? No no no. In the dark of night you will come. There are no stars in the daytime."

"They're still there," said Joanna. "You just can't see them."

"And if one cannot see them, how, pray tell, can one read them?"

We agreed to come that night, at ten o'clock.

I met Joanna outside her door at 9:59. Her mouth was set in a straight line.

"You look pretty excited for this," I joked.

"This is my excited look."

We walked upstairs in silence and knocked on Mandrake's door. *"Entrez, mes amis,"* he said from inside.

We walked in. The room reminded me of Mandrake: It

was dimly lit, everything was old, and it looked as if it had been richly decorated once, long ago. Antique maps of stars hung from the walls in rickety gold frames. A faded print of a queen surrounded by corgis sat on the mantel. Incense smoke filled the air. The only light came from the blinking red lights of the smoke detectors on every wall, and from about a dozen candles. On closer inspection, I realized the candles were small electric lights that flickered to look like candlelight.

"Further in, further in," came Mandrake's voice from some unseen spot. "Close the door. Shut the rest of the world outside. Step into starlight." Mandrake strode forward out of the shadows, clad in a purple silk robe. He waved his hands toward the ceiling. It was covered in constellations of glowing stars—tiny spots of greenish light in the dark room.

"Are those glow-in-the-dark stickers?" said Joanna.

"Hush!" said Mandrake. "Gaze upon the Milky Way. Upon the shimmering torso of Andromeda. Upon the pinching claws of Cancer—"

"The claws of what?" interrupted Joanna.

"The crab. Not the disease. Gaze upon the glorious wings of Pegasus. Orion's belt is shining. The Big Dipper is upside down over us. It's pouring out its light."

"I had those same stickers on my ceiling when I was little," whispered Joanna.

"You promised to keep quiet," I said.

"I'm trying."

"These stars are merely an echo of the real stars," said Doctor Mandrake. "Come with me, young Sea Goat. Come

with me up. And come with me out." He took me by the hand and led me back through what I guessed must be his living room. Joanna followed behind. We came to a door. Mandrake flung it open, revealing a shadowy stairway.

"Behold," said Mandrake. "The stairway to the heavens." His voice dropped to a whisper. "Watch your head, the ceiling is kind of low in here." We followed Mandrake up the narrow stairs until we stepped through a hatch, onto the roof of the Bright House. Four rusty beach loungers were spread out in the darkness.

"We have been blessed with a clear night. Witness the stars in all their glory."

"This is actually pretty cool," said Joanna. "I didn't know you could come up here."

"Thank you, my dear. It's nice to know at least one thing meets with your approval. Sea Goat, lie back on this lounge and look toward the heavens."

I lay on the chair and looked up.

"Now then," continued Mandrake. "You are a Capricorn. Do you know where your constellation lies?"

"I can barely find the Big Dipper," I said.

"Ursa Major! The great bear. We'll be staying away from her. Tonight, we look for Capricornus, the mighty Sea Goat!"

"You don't usually hear *mighty* and *goat* in the same sentence," said Joanna.

Mandrake glared at her, then turned his eyes upward. "First, we find Cygnus, the boy who was transformed into a swan. Can you see the swan there? It looks like a cross of bright stars."

"If it looks like a cross, why do they call it a swan?" asked Joanna.

"Because, unlike you, the ancients had imaginations. Yours has probably been ruined by staring at your phone too long. Now then, the bright star at the top of the cross is called Deneb. Draw an imaginary line from that through Epsilon Cygni—the bright one on the left tip of the cross. Then follow that line rather close to the horizon—and there! There it is! Capricornus the Sea Goat! Do you see it?"

"I'm still looking for the swan," I said.

Mandrake sighed and walked me through the process again and again until I finally spotted a crooked triangle that he assured me represented a goat.

"That is Capricorn there. Imagine how glorious it must have looked to the ancients. And now, thousands of years later, it still tells us what lies before you."

"Oh, brother," said Joanna. "You really believe in this mumbo jumbo?"

"I certainly believe it. And it is not, as you say, mumbo jumbo."

"I believe in science," Joanna said. Then she bit her lip. "I mean, yes, there's things that I don't understand—"

"Which is precisely the purpose of my studies," said Mandrake. "To make sense of what we don't understand. But of course, science has the same goal. Do you know, my dear, that in the ancient days—in the days of Solomon— astronomers and scientists were one and the same?"

"You mean back in the days when they thought the earth was flat?"

"And did you know that the wise men—the very wise men mentioned in the Bible—they read the stars just like me?"

"I don't believe in that stuff, either. At least—at least not most of the time."

"Ahh—you are what I like to call a *rational man*."

"I'm not a man, in case you haven't noticed. I'm a girl. And I believe what I see." She paused. "Even if sometimes I wish I'd never seen it."

"Because your so-called rational mind is closed to all that is invisible."

"Definitely."

"Yet most of the universe is invisible. The stars above our heads hold our gaze, but most of the sky is blackness. It is empty space. Do you believe in it?"

"Do I believe in what?" said Joanna.

"Do you believe in the empty space? Because you cannot see it. Now then, enough debating. Sea Goat, let's get on with your reading."

Mandrake cleared his throat and spread his arms. "You will soon make a new start, Sea Goat, if you let your heart be your guide. Your friends and family will support you in a grand way, and together you will forge new paths. It is time to leave the past in the past and press on. Remember, your effort is not failure if it doesn't work the first time. Persist, young Sea Goat! Persist!"

Mandrake bowed in my direction, as if waiting for me to applaud. I nodded from my lounger. "Umm, thanks, I guess."

"You are very welcome."

"This *is* mumbo jumbo," said Joanna. "*Forge new paths.* You could say that garbage about anyone."

"Joanna," I said, "you promised to be quiet."

"I know, but I can't help it. It's a bunch of hooey. It's so vague it means nothing. We shouldn't encourage him."

Mandrake spun toward her. "My dear young lady, you assume I depend upon your encouragement. I do not. Many more substantial beings than you have doubted my powers."

"I bet they have."

"And many came to believe. You are a Taurus. Born between April the twenty-first and May the twentieth."

"Who told you that?"

"You did, my dear, by your excessively obstinate nature. I would bet that you were born in late April around the twenty-fifth. Or perhaps a bit later."

"The twenty-seventh," said Joanna, "but that doesn't prove anything."

"It proves I'm right about two things—your astrological sign and your obstinate personality. Would you like me to do a reading for you?"

"Why bother?" said Joanna. "It'll be so vague that it could be about anyone."

"I reject the term *vague* in favor of the term *high-minded*. I prefer to keep my readings at a higher level, to allow for interpretation. To allow for wisdom. But if that is too challenging for your narrow view, I can get much more specific."

"Go for it," Joanna dared him, narrowing her eyes and pursing her lips.

"I warn you, you may not like it."

"I'll be fine. Do your worst."

Mandrake nodded, then looked up to the sky. "Taurus

the bull is easy to find. You simply follow Orion's belt—those three bright stars right there in a line."

Even I could see those stars—three bright spots lined up straight. They really did look like a belt.

"Just move up the sky along that straight line to that bright cluster. That's Taurus. That bright star in the middle is called Aldebaran. It's the bull's fiery eye. It's easier than almost any constellation to read. Most people born under Taurus are quite obvious. An open book on a starlit table, you might say."

Mandrake put his hands together. "Now then, Saturn is moving out of your relationship zone and Jupiter is moving in. That means you will make new relationships this year—either friendly or romantic, I can't quite tell. You will feel torn between your desire for independence and your longing to stay by the side of the one you love the most."

"I thought you said you were going to get specific," said Joanna.

"That was quite specific."

"That was mush."

Mandrake said, "To get more specific is not recommended."

"Cop-out. You can't do it."

"You are a difficult child. Very well." Mandrake tightened the belt around his robe. He stared first at the constellation and then at Joanna. "You will meet an old enemy on a white ship. Oh, and as much as it galls me to say so, you will come into a significant sum of money. Fifty thousand dollars. And—ohh—what is this? Hmm. Ahh . . ." Mandrake's voice trailed off.

"What?" asked Joanna.

"Nothing. I thought I saw something. It's nothing."

"You did see something. You're just not saying. What did you see?"

"It's nothing."

"What is it?"

"What difference does it make? You don't believe it, anyway."

"You're right. It makes no difference. So tell me."

Mandrake sighed. "You are forcing me. Very well. I see a woman. She is broken. Destroyed. You are standing beside her, but she is broken. Beyond repair."

"What woman?" Joanna's voice sounded small.

"A mother."

"Whose mother?"

"Your very own."

"What?" said Joanna. Her voice cracked. "Why would you say that?" A sob came out between the words. "It's not true. My mother is not broken—not beyond repair. She's—she's gonna get better. You—you—stupid phony!"

Joanna ran to the hatch and disappeared from the roof. I ran after her, then stopped and turned toward Mandrake. "You know her mom has cancer, don't you? Why'd you have to do that?"

"Why?" said Mandrake. "Because it is true."

RIGHTING WRONGS

I chased Joanna down to her apartment, but she wouldn't answer the door. Her mom did. Mrs. Sedley called for Joanna, but Joanna wouldn't come. Mrs. Sedley said, "What's going on, Gabe? Did you do something to upset her?" I didn't know how to answer the question, so I just said I'd come back later.

I texted Joanna the next morning, but she didn't reply. I even knocked on her door again, but no one answered, not even her mom. At school, I looked for her at lunch, but didn't see her. I went to language arts class a few minutes early, hoping I could talk to her before class started, but she wasn't there.

The bell rang. There was still no sign of Joanna. Or Miss Kratz. My classmates started throwing balls of paper around and checking their phones. I watched the door, hoping Miss Kratz would stay away, and hoping Joanna would show.

Suddenly the door burst open. A woman stood there.

She had blond hair, sunglasses studded with diamonds, and a floor-length fur coat. "Hello, children," she said. Only then did I realize it was Miss Kratz.

She slammed the door with a bang and walked to the front of the room. As she walked by, I noticed sparkly rings on at least half of her fingers. She wrapped the fur coat tightly around her and smiled at us. "Guess what? I'm rich."

No one said anything.

"See this coat? It's made from the hides of cute little dead animals called minks. Isn't that awful? It cost twenty-seven thousand dollars. And the jewelry on just this hand cost more than I make at this crummy school in a year. The other hand is even worse. Oh, I want to show you something—" She reached into the pockets of her coat and pulled out wads of cash. "Hundred-dollar bills. Who wants one?"

Nearly every hand in the room shot up.

"You each want one? Should I hand them out by rows or in alphabetical order? Or should I just keep them all for myself? I think I'll keep them. Do you know why? Because it's my money. Mine." She jammed the money back into her pockets and walked to her desk. She opened and closed a drawer. "I thought there'd be something here I'd miss. But guess what? There isn't. Except for all of you, of course. I'll miss you children." She grinned. "Just kidding! I won't miss you, either!"

Miss Kratz began walking slowly toward the back of the room, swinging her ring-covered hands. "If you thought you were my favorite, you probably weren't. If you thought I actually read your essays, I probably didn't. And if you thought Shakespeare was boring, I agree with you. Shakespeare *is* boring. Who talks like that? But money—money is delightful! Oh, and before I forget, I quit. If you see Principal What's-His-Face, tell him I said so."

Miss Kratz blew us a kiss, walked out, and slammed the door again.

The rest of the class period was total chaos. I couldn't help wondering where Miss Kratz had gotten her money. I couldn't help wondering if I would see her again.

Dear Reader, I would see her again, sitting on the deck of her own yacht.

I decided to go to Joanna's apartment after school. Before I went inside the Bright House, I saw Jimmy Hyde on the side of our gross, flaking building using the water hose. He was so intent on what he was doing that he didn't see me.

At his feet, Jimmy had an old coffee can filled with paintbrushes. He was carefully washing the brushes one by one in the stream of the hose. "Hey Jimmy," I said. "Been doing a little handyman work?"

Jimmy jumped. He spun around, kicking over his can of brushes as he did so. He smiled, but it didn't make his face any more appealing. He quickly gathered the brushes up and ran around the corner and into the building. I heard his door slam. I turned off the water and hung up the hose. I was tired of people running away from me and slamming doors.

When I entered the lobby, I heard Jimmy Hyde's music click off. A few seconds later, Hashimoto stepped out of her studio, closing the door quickly behind her and leaning against it. Today she was sporting a red plastic dress. She wore pure white stockings, white leather boots, and white gloves. Even her wig was white.

"Darling." She walked up and took both of my hands. "Hashimoto is delighted to see you. Where have you been hiding lately? And where is your lovely lady friend?"

"You mean Joanna?"

"That one. Don't tell me you two are having a lover's spat."

"We're not, umm—"

"I told you not to tell me! Don't tell me! I have been so busy painting today—so focused—like a terrier chasing a rat. But not an ugly rat. A beautiful rat."

"You don't really look like you've been working very hard."

Hashimoto's whole face puckered, as if she'd just bit into a lemon. "What do you mean?"

"I mean your clothes. White gloves and boots and all that. You don't have a speck of paint on you."

"Can't a woman change her clothes?"

"I didn't mean anything by it. I was just, you know, making an observation."

"Are you nosey? If I thought you were nosey, I never would have invited you into my studio."

"I'm not nosey."

"But here you are, examining my wardrobe to verify that I have been working. I thought we were friends, Gabriel Silver."

She turned and locked her studio door with a key, then marched past me.

I stood outside her door for half a minute, listening. I heard a series of small thumps, like someone was walking around inside her studio. I was nearly certain of it.

I ran up to Joanna's apartment and knocked on the door. It took a minute of knocking, but finally Joanna answered. "Would you just go away? I don't want to talk to you."

"I want to break into Hashimoto's studio," I said.

"What? What are you talking about?"

"I want to go inside her studio when she's not there."

"You an art thief now?"

"No. I just want to look around. You wanna help?"

"Why would I want to do that?"

"I don't know. I thought maybe you could use—you know—a distraction."

"From what?"

"From worrying about your mom dying."

Joanna clenched her teeth and stared at me. I was so

sure she was going to slug me that I braced myself for the pain. She said, "Let me put some shoes on."

We walked downstairs together and stood silently outside the studio door. Alejandro came out of his tiny room holding a pipe wrench and a blowtorch. He smiled at us. "Are you ever going to fix the hole in our ceiling?" I asked. Alejandro shrugged. When he left, we went back to listening at Hashimoto's door. Now I was completely certain of it. Someone or something was definitely moving inside the studio.

"Do you hear that?" I whispered. Joanna nodded.

We heard what sounded like a door opening and closing. The studio went silent.

"I think whoever it was left," said Joanna. She pulled me outside. "I wonder if there's some kind of secret door to the studio we don't know about."

Joanna and I walked around the building. Even though we'd never seen one, we looked for another door, just to be sure. We found nothing.

"I don't think we're going to be breaking in anywhere today," Joanna said.

We sat on the porch steps. "How's your mom doing?" I asked.

"Not good. For a while there, it looked like she was in full remission."

"What's that?"

"Remission means the cancer is gone. But it came back. And it's spread. To her kidneys. It's at stage four now."

"And that's bad?"

"Practically no one survives stage four. So Mandrake was right. My mother is broken beyond repair."

"Don't believe that stuff," I said.

"It's true. She's broken. And no one can fix her."

I stared at the sidewalk, my mind swirling back. "I could have."

"Could have what?"

"I could have fixed her. Could have wished for her to be cured."

"Yeah. You could have."

"You thought about it, too, huh?"

"Of course I did. You could have wished for her to get better. If I'd bought the bottle from you, I could have, too. And now she's not better. She's worse."

"But if you'd asked me to wish for that it would have been like asking me to give someone else cancer."

"How do you know that? How do you know it wouldn't just mean someone else, like, breaks their arm. Or maybe just stubs their toe. I mean, you asked for a pizza and caused a car wreck. It wasn't a one-for-one deal."

"Right, but—"

"But what?" Joanna's voice started rising. "You were afraid that by helping my mom, you might hurt someone else. But you know what? You know what really bothers me? By not helping, you still chose. You chose to let my mom die. You chose a stranger over my mom."

Joanna left. I sat alone on the porch, watching the occasional car drive by. Each car contained a stranger or two—some person I had never met. Had I chosen these people over Mrs. Sedley?

It didn't matter now. The bottle was gone. Joanna would probably hate me forever. Unless . . .

I walked slowly inside and up the stairs, arguing with myself at every step. I knocked on Joanna's door. I had to knock for more than a minute before it opened.

"What?" said Joanna.

"I want to help your mom," I said.

"Bit late for that now. The bottle's long gone."

"So let's get it back."

WE HUNT FOR THE BOTTLE

WE INVITED HENRY OVER and I explained my half-formed plan. It was simple. We'd find the Brackleys and ask to buy the bottle back.

"You think someone like Lancaster is going to part with something like that?" said Joanna.

"He might. That bottle wears on you, believe me."

"Yeah, but more likely he'll wish us to go away forever."

"I thought you wanted to save your mom," I said.

"I just don't think this is gonna work."

"You never know until you try."

So we tried. Dear Reader, it didn't take much work to find Lancaster. A simple Google search revealed four newspaper stories about the Brackleys. One was about their winning lottery ticket. Another was an investigation into their second winning ticket. The third was about Lancaster. The headline read LOCAL BOY WINS STATE TENNIS CHAMPIONSHIP.

The article told how Lancaster, an eighth grader who

somehow made the high school team near the end of the season, had won every single game on his way to the state finals. His opponents had suffered broken ankles, groin pulls, dislocated shoulders, and even a couple of car wrecks. A photo showed Lancaster holding a huge silver cup over his head.

"Jeez Louise," said Henry. "Lancaster didn't waste much time putting the old imp to work, did he?"

The fourth article was the one that really caught my eye. The headline read BRACKLEY FAMILY CONVERTS MUSEUM INTO PRIVATE RESIDENCE. The article told how Danny and Goody Brackley, who had a son, Lancaster, had purchased a historic mansion that housed the Sullivan History Museum. They had fired the staff, cleared out the exhibits, and moved into the building. The article quoted one of the neighbors, who referred to the Brackleys as "the most hated family in Tacoma."

I found the address for the mansion. It was three-thirty when we climbed onto the number fourteen bus and headed west. The bus dropped us off about a mile from Lancaster's address. We walked. A quarter mile before we came to the house, we could already see it.

It was huge, standing up on a hill overlooking the Puget Sound, surrounded by a black wrought-iron fence. At the main gate we were greeted by a voice coming out of a speaker. We gave our names, and a minute later the gate swung open and the voice told us to walk up to the main house.

A man in a suit answered the door. He introduced himself as Gherkin and said he would get Lancaster for us.

A minute later, the door opened and Lancaster smiled at me. "Man, Silver, it sure is good to see a familiar face." I introduced him to Henry and reminded him of Joanna's name.

Lancaster wore a brand-new Adidas tracksuit, with a couple of pounds of gold chains hanging around his neck. He was thin. His hair was shaggy and his skin was pale. He led us inside the mansion. It was huge. Just the entryway was as big as my family's entire apartment. Beyond that, I saw a living room—if that's what you call it in a mansion—that must have been a hundred feet in each direction.

It was hard to notice much else about the mansion, because the place was jammed with so much stuff. Leather couches, chairs, tables, TVs, lamps, and every other type of furniture you could imagine filled every inch of the place, just as it had filled their little apartment at the Bright House.

Lancaster didn't seem to notice. He led us over and around the furniture, climbing across a sofa and table without comment. We followed after until we came to a couple of couches facing each other. We sat down, with our feet on the couches, as there was no visible floor to put them on. "So what's up with you guys? How's life back at the old dump?" I noticed his hands shook while he spoke.

"About the same." I said. "How's life here?"

"What do you think?" said Lancaster. "I mean, does it get any better than this? I'm probably the richest kid in America. Or one of them."

"How's your mom and dad?"

"Goody left. I gave her a couple of million and told her to take a hike. I'm not sure where Dad is these days. New York, last I heard. So I have this whole awesome place to myself. Hey, you guys want to play some video games? You should see how big my TV is."

I cleared my throat. "Actually, Lancaster, I came to talk to you about the bottle."

"I don't want it."

"Wow. Really? That's perfect, because—"

"Do we have to talk about it? Wouldn't you rather see my stereo collection? I've got a whole room full of nothing but stereos."

"I wanna see them," said Henry. "That sounds amazing."

"I have one set of speakers so loud that I can actually

blow the glass out of the windows. Come to think of it, we probably can't go in that room right now."

"Lancaster, we really need to talk about—"

"Hey, did I tell you about my zoo? I have a lion."

Joanna said, "You have a lion? In a cage?"

"In a cage? That's a good idea. And I have two zebras— or maybe only one now. And a boa constrictor and twelve monkeys."

"I love monkeys," said Henry.

"I have an octopus, too. I keep it in the pool."

"You have a pool?"

"'Course I have a pool. That reminds me, Silver. Did you ever get my going-away present? The hot tub?"

"That was you?"

"Sure was. Bought it for you with my lottery winnings. Knew you'd love it. You're welcome."

"Yeah. Thanks. But can we stay focused on the bottle? That's why we're here."

Lancaster frowned. "I said already that I don't want it."

"That's perfect."

"Don't get me wrong. My life is awesome. Awesome house. All this awesome stuff. Awesome octopus. But it weighs on you—the bottle. You know what I mean?"

"I sure do," I said.

"And it's too much for—well, for me. For someone like me. Cause I—I can't resist it."

"Then you shouldn't have it," I said.

"I know. I shouldn't. I can't. Because you were right, Silver. That thing is bad news. Do you know what it made me do? Do you know how many people I've hurt?" He paused as a stream of monkey chittering echoed through the house. "The truth is I'm all alone in this place. My step-mom left. She left. I didn't kick her out. My dad is afraid to come home. I hired servants, but they kept getting hurt whenever I'd wish for something. The only person who's willing to stick around is Gherkin. You know why? I pay him a hundred thousand dollars each month, just so he doesn't leave."

Henry gulped. "A hundred thousand? For a month? Hey, maybe I could stick around for a few weeks." Joanna el-bowed him in the side. "Ouch," said Henry. "I was only kid-ding. But how much would you pay for a sleepover?"

I said, "Lancaster, if you don't want the bottle, then sell it back to me."

"What? I thought you had it and were trying to sell it to *me* again."

"You mean you don't have it?"

"No way. Haven't you been listening? It was hurting people. So I sold it. And good riddance. I still have all this stuff. And tons of money. And I still get to keep—you know, my soul."

Joanna leaned forward. "Who'd you sell it to?"

"Some guy named—oh, what was his name. Cavendish, I think. The guy who used to clean the pool."

Joanna said, "Do you know where we can find him?"

"I think Gherkin knows him. I'll have him drive you."

I thanked Lancaster. I looked at his pale skin and shaky hands. "You wanna come along?" I said.

"Me? No. I don't leave the house. Too dangerous out there. Someone like Cavendish might make a wish for one of my cars. That could kill me. I'm staying here."

"What if they wish for your whole house?" said Henry.

"Shut up! Shut up! Just wait outside, would you? Gherkin will meet you out there."

JOANNA MAKES HER ONLY WISH

GHERKIN DROVE US IN A LONG WHITE LIMOUSINE and dropped us off about seven miles away, at a huge house in Lakewood, right on the shore of American Lake. The house had one of those sweeping driveways. It was loaded with fancy cars.

I knocked on the door, but a maid told us that Mr. Cavendish was out of town. She said he'd be back the next day. I left her my name and phone number on a piece of paper and said, "Be sure to tell him it's about the bottle."

We began walking home. The Cavendish house was half a mile from the nearest bus stop, and then we had to take three buses before we were within walking distance of the Bright House. The trip took more than two hours.

We were rounding the corner on our block when my cell phone rang. I answered and put it on speakerphone. It was Cavendish. His voice was rough. There was a lot of noise in the background. "I'm calling from Chicago. At the airport. You left a message about a bottle?"

"I'm a former owner," I said.

"So am I," said Cavendish.

"You mean you don't have it?"

"I only kept it for a weekend. Cleared a few million bucks. Got a bunch of cars and a couple of houses. Got a business—a chain of drugstores. Then I sold it—the bottle, I mean. Gave me the heebie-jeebies. Kept thinking I was going to get hit by a bus and be damned to hell forever."

"Who'd you sell it to?" I said.

"It was a lot harder than I thought. Took me ten tries to find someone who would take it. Finally sold it to one of my former schoolteachers." Cavendish gave me a name I recognized: Miss Kratz. Our language arts teacher.

"So that's how she got so rich," I said. A question entered my mind. I asked it. "How much did you buy it for?"

"Six cents," said Cavendish.

"Six?" my heart sank. "I sold it to Lancaster for ninety-nine cents. Why did he sell it to you for six?"

"It was all I had on me."

I hung up.

Dear Reader, believe me when I say I felt sick to my stomach. The bottle imp was only four sales away from the final owner—the owner whose soul would be claimed by the Devil. No wonder it was so hard for Cavendish to sell.

I called the school. They wouldn't give me Miss Kratz's information, so I fired up Mom's laptop and Googled Miss Kratz's address. It took me awhile, because I don't think most teachers like their contact info in the hands of their students, but I eventually found two addresses. One was a house a few miles away. The other address was listed as Slip F-18, Tyee Marina.

"She lives at a marina?" said Henry.

"Of course she does," said Joanna, "if she wished for a boat. It's probably a big one. Let's try there first."

Forty-five minutes later, we leaned our bikes against the gate of Tyee Marina. The gate was locked, but we eventually managed to sneak in behind another visitor.

We made our way to Slip F-18 and found Miss Kratz lying in a deck chair on the back of a huge white yacht. It was early June in Tacoma, but she was wearing a bikini.

"That is a sight I had no desire to see," whispered Henry.

I knocked on the railing and said hello. Miss Kratz yawned. A lazy hand lifted her sunglasses. Her head jerked back when she recognized the three of us. "What are you kids doing here?" Her other hand groped about for her beach towel. She covered herself and sat up.

"We came to talk about the bottle."

"The—the what? The bottle? What bottle?"

"The one you wished on. The one that got you all of this."

Miss Kratz's tan seemed to fade. "I have no idea what you're talking about."

"It's okay," I said. "I used to own it. I sold it to a kid named Lancaster Brackley. He sold it to a guy named Cavendish. Cavendish told us he sold it to you."

Miss Kratz stared at me. "And where did you get it?"

"From an old man named Shoreby. You may have heard of him. He used to be the richest man in Tacoma."

"Used to be?"

"Now he's dead."

"What do you mean by *dead*?"

Joanna stepped forward. "He means dead. Like in a coffin six feet underground. Shoreby sold the bottle just in time to keep his immortal soul from going to the Devil—"

"Don't say that!" Miss Kratz tightened the towel around herself. "There's no need to bring all that up."

"But you know the rules, right?"

"I know them! I know them. Look, don't you kids have somewhere else you need to be? I'm not your teacher anymore. No one's paying me to be nice to you."

"But we're here to help," said Joanna. "We're here to keep the Devil from getting your soul."

Miss Kratz lifted her sunglasses again. "Yeah? And just how would you do that? Do you know what my plan was for this bottle? I told myself I'd only own it for a couple of days. Wish myself a few million dollars. Quit my job. Buy a boat. And then dump it before anything—you know—bad happens to me. Well I've tried to sell the thing a dozen times. You'd think it would be easy. I mean, look at my life. Look at what I own."

"Then what's the trouble? Why isn't anyone buying?"

"Turns out people care more about their souls than you'd think. And there are only a few sales left in it. I bought it from Cavendish for five cents. And I can't find anyone who'll buy it for four. It's too close to—to the you-know-what."

"The Devil," said Joanna.

"Stop—saying—that," said Miss Kratz. "You are a rude girl, Joanna. I never liked you."

"I never liked you, either," said Joanna, "but I'll buy the bottle right now."

"Wait a sec!" said Henry. "Joanna, didn't you hear what she just said? She can't find anyone to buy it for four cents. When you sell it, you'll have to find someone who will buy it for three. What if you get stuck with it?"

"Don't listen to him." Miss Kratz reached into a bag right beside her deck chair. "I'll sell it. I have it right here."

"I want it," said Joanna.

"No!" said Henry. "You can't do it!"

Joanna pushed Henry away from her. She dug into her pocket and pulled out a handful of coins. She held out four pennies to Miss Kratz. "I even have exact change."

Miss Kratz looked at her. "You're so young."

"I'm old enough to know what I'm doing."

"Then get a boat," said Miss Kratz. "The boat is real nice. I like the boat. You already know the rules?"

Joanna nodded. Miss Kratz said the words that made the bottle Joanna's. Joanna handed over the four pennies. As soon as she held the bottle in her hands, she said, "I wish that my mom would be cured of her cancer. Right now."

Miss Kratz grabbed Joanna by her arm. "That's what you wanted? To help your mom? You could have just asked me to wish for you."

"Asked you? To help me? You're serious?"

"'Course I'm serious. I'm not that bad. Am I?"

"You're not exactly Mother Teresa. But I couldn't ask. Not even you," said Joanna. She met my eyes before continuing. "I know how this thing works. I know that some-one else might get hurt. That's bad enough. I couldn't add to that by making you hurt someone for me. I can barely stand to do it myself. At least this way I've also freed you."

"I'm sorry," said Miss Kratz. "Oh, I'm so sorry." Then she giggled. "But I am free from it, aren't I? I'm free from the bottle, and I get to keep my soul. And my boat." She giggled some more. It was creepy. There was nothing funny, but she just kept giggling away. She was still giggling when we left.

Joanna tucked the bottle into the pocket of her jeans. We climbed onto our bikes and rode back to the Bright

House. My hands were shaking so much it was hard to ride. I think we were all desperate to see if Joanna's mom was feeling better. But I was nervous about Joanna being stuck with that bottle.

When we reached the building, we piled our bikes onto the sidewalk without locking them and pounded up the stairs. Joanna opened the door and we pushed into her apartment.

Mrs. Sedley's body lay sprawled out on the living room floor.

THE PORTRAIT

JOANNA FELL TO THE GROUND by her mother's body. "Mom!" She grabbed Mrs. Sedley's shoulders and began shaking her.

Mrs. Sedley's eyes opened wide. "Joanna? What's wrong?" she said. She looked around the apartment from her position on the floor of the living room. "Oh, I see. You thought—oh, honey, I'm so sorry."

"Why are you down here?"

"I don't know." She squinted at her watch. "About half an hour ago I was doing a little cleaning, and then I grew suddenly tired. And the floor just looked so comfortable. I just wanted to lie down. I must have fallen asleep." She yawned. "It was a delicious nap until you started shaking me."

"Half an hour ago," said Joanna. "That's about right. But how do you feel now?"

"Me? Fine."

"No, seriously. How do you really feel?"

"I feel fine, honey. Now quit cross-examining me. You'd

think I was the child and you were the mom. But I'm the mom. And this mom is . . . well, this mom is going to cook something. What sounds good?"

"I don't know."

"How about pancakes? You boys want some pancakes?"

"Heck yes," said Henry.

"Pancakes it is." Mrs. Sedley stood up. She stretched, then noticed we were all staring at her.

"What are you looking at? I'm fine." She walked into the kitchen.

I whispered, "How do we know if she's really better?"

Joanna shrugged. "Probably need doctors and stuff to know for sure. But she seems a little better, doesn't she?"

I could hear Mrs. Sedley singing in the kitchen. Yes. She seemed better.

Later that night, I texted with Joanna.

Well?

> I think she's better. It's hard to tell. She just ordered a bunch of Chinese food for dinner.

After all those pancakes?

> She said she was still hungry.

Is that good?

> I think so.

When are you going to sell the bottle?

> Not until I make sure that she's really better.

Over the next few days, Joanna continued to update me on her mom's progress. She told me Mrs. Sedley was sleeping better, eating more, and starting to take walks around the neighborhood.

At the end of the week, school ended for the summer, but, Dear Reader, believe me when I say I barely noticed. On that same day, Joanna made her mom go in for a checkup, even though she wasn't scheduled to have one for another week. Joanna had to beg the doctors to give her mom a head-to-toe exam.

"They thought I was crazy," she said to me. "I said I wouldn't leave until they tested her for everything. I think the only reason they agreed to do all the tests was to calm me down."

"And?"

"And all the tests showed the same thing."

"What? They showed what?"

Joanna smiled. "No more cancer."

"None?"

"None. They still want to monitor, of course. She's still got to come in a bunch of times. And I mean a bunch. But the doctor said that not only is the cancer gone, but her blood looks great, she's gained some weight, and even her heart rate is down."

"That's amazing. Now you can sell the bottle."

"Now I can," said Joanna, but the smile had left her face.

The next day—the first real day of summer vacation—I saw Mandrake in the stairway. He pulled himself up each step with a groan. He was unshaven and his silk robe was untied. The sash dragged on the steps. He saw me and said, "Oh, Sea Goat. Would you consider helping me up to my apartment? I am exhausted, dear boy. Completely exhausted. Perhaps you could walk behind me and push. Oh, why did I ever get the unit on the top floor?"

I pushed and pulled Mandrake while he groaned and wheezed. We finally reached his apartment. He collapsed into the nearest chair. I said, "Are you sick?"

"If I'm not, I soon will be. I haven't slept in days. You don't have that dreadful bottle again, do you?"

"Actually, I wanted to talk to you about that—"

Mandrake mopped his sweaty forehead with the end of his sash. "I knew it. Sea Goat, be done with that thing before you kill me."

"Is there any chance you'd want it? To buy it?"

"Dear boy, you couldn't pay me to take it."

"But what about one of your customers? Don't you buy and sell antiques?"

He steadied his gaze at me. "I have a very select list of clientele. And there is not one of them—" He paused. "No. Not even old Mrs. Hoover. There is not one I would burden with that accursed object. Get it out of the building. Out out out! Before I die of exhaustion."

I went downstairs and joined Henry and Joanna on the front steps of the Bright House, trying to think of someone—anyone—we could sell the bottle to.

"What about Dave?" said Henry.

"Who's Dave?"

"You know. Dave. The guy with the cheese shop. He buys and sells cheese, right? Maybe he'd buy this."

"I don't think we should sell it to anyone we like."

"Why?"

"Because if it's hard to sell now, think about how much harder it would be for Dave to sell. He'd buy it for three cents, but then he'd have to sell it for two. Who would buy it for two cents, knowing they'd have to convince the next person to buy it for a single penny? That's the last deal. That last person will lose their soul."

"Assuming any of that is even true," said Joanna.

"Is your mom better?" I said.

"Yes."

"And remember when the imp came out of the bottle?"

Joanna didn't answer, but she put her injured thumb in her mouth.

"Hey, I have an idea," said Henry. "What if you sold it for less, but not a whole cent less? Like maybe Joanna could sell it for three-point-five cents or three-point-nine cents." Henry stood to his feet. "Or maybe three-point-nine-nine-nine cents. I mean, you could keep selling it practically forever if you did that."

"You can't do that, remember?" I said. "Shoreby said you had to sell it for a whole coin less, and that the last person stuck with it would be when it was at one cent."

"So she should *wish* to be able to sell it for less than a cent, then."

"Did you listen to anything Shoreby said?" I asked. "You can't wish to change the rules."

Joanna sighed. "So there's three deals left. After all these years. After who knows how many people."

"Think of how many people have gotten rich from it," said Henry.

"Think how many have gotten hurt by it," said Joanna.

"Yeah," I said. "I wonder if we'll ever find out."

"Find out what?"

"You know—who paid the price. For your mom getting cured."

Joanna shook her head. "Do you ever think that sometimes we'd all be better off if you just kept your mouth shut?"

"What if you're stuck with it, Joanna?"

"It's fine. I knew what I was getting into. It was my decision."

"Yeah, but I mean, stuck with it forever?"

"I know what you meant. I'll figure it out."

"But what if you don't?"

Joanna slugged me in the arm—in the same spot where she always hit me. "Geez, Gabe, would you just shut up and give it a rest?"

A red Lincoln Town Car pulled up to the curb. Hashimoto stepped out of the backseat and walked by us, dressed from head to toe in black and white zebra stripes with a pure white cape.

"Darlings," she said, as she approached the steps. "How are my dears today? Ahh, why do you all look so sad? Hashimoto does not like these frowny faces. You all look as if you just found out your Louis Vuitton luggage was lost by the airline. Stop all this frowning. Now let me by. I have painting to do."

Hashimoto walked up the stairs and into her studio. When she closed the door, her white cape caught. She must have tugged on it from the other side, because the end of it slipped out of sight. As it did so, the door to her studio opened a crack. Light shone out. I looked at Joanna. She'd seen, too.

"What?" said Henry. "What's going on? Is that the crazy genius lady you talked about?"

"Her door's open," I said.

"Duh. I see that. So what?"

"So this is our chance to see what she is actually painting!"

"I thought you told me you'd been inside there before," Henry said.

"I have," I said, "but she always keeps her paintings covered up. Wrapped in cloth. That's her whaddayacallit— her style."

"Her gimmick," said Joanna. She crept toward the door.

Henry and I followed.

The barely cracked door gave such a tiny view that only one of us could look in at a time. Joanna looked first. "What do you see?" I whispered.

"Shhh. . . . I can't really tell. Oh, wait, there's Hashimoto. I can't tell what she's doing. She's got something in her hand. Looks like a set of keys. Yeah. She's unlocking something."

"Can you see any of the paintings?"

"Not really. I'm gonna open the door a little more."

"She'll see you!" I said.

"Who cares? She's just an artist. It's not like she's dangerous." Joanna opened the door a tiny bit more. I could see in now, over her shoulder, but from my angle, all I saw were paintings on easels, wrapped in cloth. Joanna opened the door a few more inches. Then, before I could stop her, she dropped to her knees and crawled inside.

I felt my heart beating faster. Then I felt Henry's hands on my back, pushing me. He pushed me right through the door. I quickly got on all fours and followed Joanna. She crept behind a row of canvases leaning against a wall. She slipped out of sight. Henry and I followed. When Henry tried to squeeze in behind me, he knocked one of the canvases over. It fell with a thud. I held my breath.

I heard footsteps coming our way. Hashimoto came into view as she walked straight to the studio door. I watched as she pulled it open and stuck her head outside. "Hello? Darlings? Are you out there?" She looked from side to side, then closed the door and locked it with a key. She put the ring of keys into the pocket of her white cape and walked back out of my line of sight.

"Now we're trapped!" I said.

"Shhh," said Joanna. She crawled to the other end of the row of canvases. I pushed up next to her and could just see out into the studio.

"What's going on?" said Henry. "I can't see anything but your butts."

Joanna kicked out with her foot. Henry grunted, but quit talking.

Hashimoto was still dressed in her white cape and zebra stripes. She walked to a wall and pulled out her keys. She placed a key in the wall and turned it.

A panel swung open. Hashimoto walked through it. She said a few words in Japanese. A man's voice answered back. "Did you hear that?" said Joanna. I nodded.

"What do you see?" said Henry. "I'm trapped back here in buttland."

Before I could answer, we heard music—that same Hawaiian music we always heard.

"That's Jimmy Hyde's music," I said.

I heard the voices again from the other room. The man's voice grew louder. He stepped into view in mid-sentence. It was Jimmy Hyde speaking. Hashimoto stood next to him. I heard Joanna draw in her breath.

Jimmy was dressed in work clothes. He pulled a paint-splattered apron off a wall and wrapped it around himself, all the while chatting away in Japanese.

"Why is Jimmy Hyde dressed as a painter?" I said.

Hashimoto kissed Jimmy, right on his lips, then exited through the panel.

"Oh my gosh," said Joanna. "She kissed him!"

"What's happening?" said Henry.

"Shhh!"

Jimmy grabbed a box of paints and a can of brushes. He walked over to the biggest painting in the studio, set down his tools, and began unwrapping the cloth. The painting was angled just out of view. We still couldn't see it. But we could see Jimmy Hyde. He stared at the painting. He squeezed paints onto a palette. Then he set to work.

"Jimmy Hyde is painting. Why is *he* painting?" I said. "Where's Hashimoto?"

We watched in silence for a few minutes as Jimmy touched brushes to different sections of the unseen creation.

"I want to see what he's making," said Joanna. She scanned the room, then set off, crawling from easel to easel.

Henry pushed up next to me. We watched as Joanna reached a position where she could see Jimmy Hyde's work. She leaned out to look. Even from where I crouched, I could see Joanna's eyes grow wide. She got to her feet.

"Oh no!" said Henry. "What is she doing? She's gonna get us all caught."

"Hey!" shouted Joanna as she marched toward Jimmy Hyde. "What do you think you're doing?"

Jimmy spun around, dropping his palette and splattering paint over the floor. He yelled as Joanna descended upon him.

The panel in the wall opened. Hashimoto shouted in Japanese as she ran back into the studio, still dressed in her zebra stripes.

"Stop painting her!" shouted Joanna. *"You have no right!"* She grabbed Jimmy's hand. It still held a paintbrush in it, glistening with bright red paint. They fought over the brush as Hashimoto rushed toward them.

"Interloper!" shouted Hashimoto. "This is my studio! Out! Out!"

Joanna kept struggling with Jimmy Hyde. "Not without that painting!" She yanked the brush out of his hand. When she jerked it back, she flung red paint right across Hashimoto's zebra-striped dress. Hashimoto gasped, then made a sort of growling sound. She stomped forward and grabbed the painting at the same time as Joanna. The two of them began a tug-of-war.

"Give it to me!" shouted Joanna.

"Not on your life!" said Hashimoto. "It's mine!"

"Not this one," cried Joanna. "Not ever! Help!"

"Oh boy," I muttered, then sprang out of my hiding place. I could hear Henry behind me. We grabbed onto the painting. Hashimoto and Jimmy Hyde stood on the other side, pulling in their direction. Hashimoto yelled at us in Japanese.

While I fought to hang on, I just managed to get a look at the painting. It was a portrait of Joanna's mom. It was so perfectly rendered that for a second I thought it was a photograph. In the portrait, Mrs. Sedley stood in her window, staring down on the street. Her eyes glistened, as if on the verge of tears. The skin around her eyes was dark. A scarf covered her head.

"Pull hard," said Joanna. We pulled. *"Harder!"* yelled Joanna.

The three of us gave a mighty heave. We jerked the painting free. We tumbled backwards across the studio, knocking into two other easels and sending their contents flying. Henry lost his footing and fell to the ground. I fell after him, dragging the painting with me.

The framed canvas smashed over Henry's head. I heard canvas tear and wood crack. I lost my grip and fell on top of Henry and the painting, tearing it even more.

My head took a few seconds to clear. Joanna and Hashimoto stood above us, staring down at the destroyed work of art. "My beautiful painting!" Hashimoto wailed. "You've broken her. She is broken beyond repair!"

I MAKE A DECISION

WE PULLED THE BROKEN PAINTING of Joanna's mother off of Henry. And, Dear Reader, you'd think that I would have felt embarrassed. But Joanna was so mad there was no room in that studio for my feelings.

"I'm glad we broke it," Joanna said, glaring at Hashimoto. "That's my mom. Not yours. My mom, when she was dying. You didn't even ask."

Hashimoto picked up the broken painting as if it were her own sick child. "Hundreds of hours. Maybe thousands. It was to be my greatest work."

"*Your* greatest work?" said Joanna. "You didn't even paint it. I bet he did the whole thing." She pointed at Jimmy Hyde.

"I wonder if I could stitch it back together," said Hashimoto.

"I won't let you," said Joanna. "I'm taking it with me when I leave. You don't get to keep it."

Hashimoto looked down at Joanna. She sighed, then

sprawled on the floor. "It's true, you know. I didn't paint it. I didn't paint any of them. Jimmy paints them all."

"Figures," said Joanna. "He does all the work, and you take all the credit. I hope you at least pay him."

"Pay him? I don't pay him. He is not my employee. He is my husband."

"You're married?"

"Of course we are married. I love him. How could I not love him? Look at this." She stroked the torn canvas where Mrs. Sedley's image stared out.

"Then why don't you tell everyone that he does the work, so he could get the credit?"

Jimmy sat next to Hashimoto. He took her hand in his, then shook his head at us. "I've tried," she said, "but he made me promise not to. He prefers to be anonymous. Don't you, my dear?"

Jimmy smiled and nodded. He said, "Anonymous," in a voice just above a croak.

"My anonymous genius. He says that his joy is in the work. In the doing. And my joy is in—well, in the appearance of it all." She kissed Jimmy's hand. "I am beautiful on the outside. My Jimmy is beautiful on the inside."

She laughed. "My married name is not even Hashimoto. It is Mrs. Hyde. Hitomi Hyde. But that's not a name that sells out shows. You know, I've been an artist for years and years. Doing this very same thing. This wrapping of things. But it was all flat. All dead. Until I met my Jimmy. He was painting for tourists in Hawaii, on a sidewalk in Waikiki—the most beautiful paintings you've ever seen. Done on old scraps of cardboard or plywood. But genius work even still. No one seemed to care what I wrapped up until there was something truly beautiful inside. As soon as I wrapped up one of Jimmy's beautiful paintings, it gave off a strange kind of power. You couldn't see his painting in there—all the meticulous brush strokes and—and the way he captured life—but you could feel it, right through my layers of cloth and rope." She faced us. "You'll keep our secret?"

"I guess so," I said. "I mean, those people at your gallery show were buying your wrapping as much as his paintings. That's part of the power, right?"

Hashimoto smiled. "Yes, darling. That is part of the power."

"So you're the one who likes the Hawaiian music, aren't you?"

"What?"

"The music. The Hawaiian music."

"Yes. That's me. I grew up in Honolulu. I listen to the music while he works."

I studied the painting. I remembered where I'd seen that image before—way back when we first moved in. I'd seen Mrs. Sedley looking down from her window and had caught Jimmy Hyde looking up at her, his notebook and pencil in hand.

Jimmy helped Hashimoto to her feet. Hashimoto made a slight bow toward Joanna. "I am sorry we painted your mother without asking. I didn't think it would matter, since no one was ever supposed to see it. Take it and go, with my apologies. But go."

Joanna picked up the painting. We left.

No one else was home when I returned to our apartment. Mom and Dad had taken the girls to an ice-cream social at their elementary school, so I thought I would be home alone. When I went inside, I found Alejandro on a stepladder.

"What are you doing?" I said.

Alejandro motioned to the hole in the ceiling. He had patched most of it with a piece of Sheetrock and was now smoothing wet plaster over the patch.

"I'll have you fixed up here in no time," said Alejandro.

"That hole's been there for months," I said, "if that's what you mean by *no time.*"

Alejandro shrugged. "I would have fixed it sooner, but Mrs. Appleyard requested that I not do so."

"Why?"

"You only paid extra for the leaky pipes. You didn't pay extra for the ceiling. Repairs take much longer when you don't pay extra. That's how life works in America. The home of the brave and the land where nothing is free. I just do what I'm told. I cannot afford to get in trouble with Mrs. Appleyard."

"Why don't you quit and get a better job?" I asked. "Seems like you're good at fixing everything."

"I have no papers," said Alejandro. "As long as I work for her, I get to stay in America. If I quit, Mrs. Appleyard promises to turn me in to the government. They will send me back to my country or perhaps even put me in jail."

"That's rotten," I said.

"Those are my options. Mrs. Appleyard gave them to me." He slathered more plaster onto his ceiling patch. His cell phone rang. He answered it, listened for a few seconds, then hung up. "It's Mrs. Appleyard. She says she needs me right away. Says she forgot to tell me something. Something urgent." He looked at the ceiling. "All fixed. I'll let that dry for a day or so and then come back and paint it." He carried his ladder and tools into the hall.

Dear Reader, it was the last time he would enter our apartment. The patch would never be painted.

When he left, I stared at his work. For some reason, it made me think of Mrs. Sedley. Maybe because she'd been in need of repair, too. Maybe because she'd had to wait so long. But now she was fixed. Joanna had fixed her. Maybe at the cost of her own soul. Maybe at the cost of someone else's life.

And then the reading of Doctor Mandrake zoomed out of some back corner of my head. It finally made sense to me.

I ran over to Joanna's apartment and pounded on her door. When she answered, I dragged her into the hallway. The words gushed out of my mouth. "Mandrake. His prophecy or whatever you call it. His thing about you. About you standing over the woman. Don't you see?"

"What are you talking about?" said Joanna.

"It's—it's the thing. With Hashimoto. It's not some stranger."

Joanna slugged me in the arm. "Would you just stop blathering like an idiot?"

"Oh, don't you get it? What was it that Mandrake said? About you?"

"You know what he said. About my mom. Broken beyond repair."

"Right. And you were what? Standing over her, right? I'm positive that's what he said."

"So?"

"So you're the one who's being an idiot. Don't you get it? It just happened. In Hashimoto's studio. But it wasn't your actual mother. It was a painting of her. And she—I mean the painting—was broken."

"Beyond repair," said Joanna. "Oh my gosh. You're right, Gabe. So Mandrake was right after all."

"Yeah, but who cares about that. That's not why I'm telling you."

"Then what?"

"Don't you get it? It's the price."

"The what?"

"The trade-off. You know. With the bottle. If one person wins, someone else has to lose. Your mom was fixed, right? So another mom had to be broken."

"So Hashimoto is the one who paid?" Joanna blinked a few times, then turned her face away from me. "Do you really think that settles it? That—I mean—that no one else will, you know, get hurt?"

"I'm sure of it."

Joanna wiped her eyes with her sleeve, then turned back toward me, smiling. "Then that takes care of that."

"Now we just have to figure out how to—"

"Oh, shut up, Gabe. I know. I have to sell the bottle before I lose my soul. I get it. You don't have to keep saying it over and over, like you're worried that I'd forgotten about it. It's all I think about. I get it. Okay? I get it." She stomped back into her apartment and slammed the door.

Joanna could be such a pain. But she was the only one I knew who had gotten the bottle and not wished for something stupid. No boats. No Ferraris. No pizza. No hot tubs. No giant houses. She'd only wished for her mom to get better.

Everyone else seemed to have escaped, but now Joanna was stuck with the bottle. What if she couldn't sell it? What if something happened to her? What if she died before this all got figured out?

As I stood in the hallway, staring at her door, I decided.

I didn't decide because I'm a hero or anything. Not because I'm more selfless than other people. I think it was more that I was tired of worrying about Joanna and her soul. Somehow, it would be easier if I were worrying about my own.

ONE PENNY

I walked up to Joanna's apartment door again and had my hand out to knock. I stopped. I knew she'd never sell it to me. Not in a million years. I'd ask. She'd say no. I'd beg. She'd tell me to shut up and go home. Somewhere in there she'd slug me. I rubbed the sore spot on my arm again.

Another idea struck me. I did the math in my head, let out my breath, and went down to the first floor. I knocked on Alejandro's door.

He opened it. His eyes were wide and beads of sweat covered his forehead. I asked if I could come inside. He frowned. He looked around the lobby as if making sure no one was watching, then let me in.

I knew his apartment would be small, but I didn't expect it to be so—so beautiful. It was the only word that really fit. The whole place reminded me of the cabin on a yacht, if you made a yacht out of wood scraps.

The ceiling of the room sloped down in steps, because

the room was under the stairs. The walls were paneled in intricate squares of wood, perfectly fitted together and then sanded and oiled so smooth and shiny that I swear I could almost see my reflection. Crowded bookshelves and ornate cabinets made use of every bit of space. The wooden furniture gleamed. A small table, inlaid with designs, was built into one wall. The space where the stair-ceiling went down to the ground was filled by a narrow bed that looked snug but comfortable. The floor was mostly covered in woven carpets that felt cushy under my feet. On the walls, the only interruptions to all that beautiful wood were the smoke detectors. They were in there, too.

"Wow," I said.

"You like it?"

"It's very nice."

"Thank you. I'll be sad to see it go."

Then I noticed the suitcases on the floor, half-filled with clothes and tools. "You're leaving?"

"Right now. You should go and pack, too. The day has finally come." He turned from me to move some books into one of the suitcases.

"Alejandro, hold on a sec. I need to talk to you about something."

"I can't stop," he said. "The schedule." He looked at his watch.

"What schedule? This will only take a minute." Before he could answer, I plowed into my story, telling Alejandro I had an offer for him—one that would help me out, but that could help him out, too. I told him everything, starting all the way back with meeting Mr. Shoreby and ending with Joanna's predicament—being stuck with the bottle. At first, he kept packing and checking his watch while I talked. A minute in, he stopped packing and drew a cross necklace out from under his shirt and kissed it.

I pulled five pennies out of my pocket. I handed three of them to Alejandro and said, "So here's my offer: You buy the bottle from Joanna for three cents, and then I promise to buy it from you for two. When you have it, you can wish for whatever you want. Wish for a million dollars if you like, so you can get away from Mrs. Appleyard. Wish for U.S. citizenship. I guarantee you'll get whatever you ask for."

"And when I get what I want, then someone else will lose?"

"It seems that way. It seems like—you know—like some kind of scale has to balance out."

His nose twitched and his eyes grew wide. "Do you smell smoke?" I shook my head no. Alejandro said, "It is this story, then. I thought the building was on fire, but I realize I'm smelling the smoke of hell on this situation." He kissed his cross again. "I sell it back to you for two cents, but then what? Then you'll be stuck with it. If the girl cannot find anyone to buy it for three cents, how will you find anyone to buy it for one?"

I shrugged.

Alejandro said, "You are going to be stuck with it, then you'll die and the Devil will get your soul. Why would you want to do this?"

"That's my business."

"Perhaps you have not thought this through. You are just a child."

"I've thought it through. I know what it means."

Alejandro shook his head. "You picked a crazy day to make such an offer. But I have no more time to argue. If I buy this for you and you cheat me—if you do not buy it back from me—I think God will strike you dead."

"I wouldn't be surprised," I said. "I won't cheat you."

He checked his watch one more time. "Wait here." Alejandro took my three cents and left.

I waited. I half hoped he'd come back without the bottle in his hand. I sniffed to see if I could smell smoke, too.

Almost half an hour later, Alejandro pushed through the door in a rush. "I did it! She didn't believe me at first. And then it took a long time to convince her. Too long. But I did. Finally. When I left, the girl was weeping like a baby. I think she will sleep well tonight." He held the bottle out to me. "Now you just need to buy it back. And quickly."

"Sure. But before you return it to me, you should make some wishes with it. Wish for riches. For a million dollars. For a house. Whatever you'd like."

Alejandro smiled, his watery eyes even wetter than usual. "I might have accidentally wished for a truck while I was walking down the stairs just now. I've always wanted a nice truck." He held out the bottle. "But now I only want to be rid of this. For the sake of my soul."

I stared at the bottle. I was supposed to take it. I'd promised I would. But what if I didn't? Right then, at that moment, I was still free.

"Hurry," Alejandro said. He tapped his finger on the nearest smoke alarm. "The schedule."

I felt the pennies in my pocket.

He said, "Buy it back from me. You swore you would!"

"I know. I know, I know. Just give me a minute."

"We do not have a minute," said Alejandro. His shoulders slumped. "You poor child. Perhaps I should just keep it. I'm old and won't get much more happiness in this life. As for the next—"

"Oh, give the stupid thing to me!" I said. I pulled out two pennies and threw them on his floor. Then I grabbed the bottle.

"I sell it to you, then!" shouted Alejandro. *"I bless you, boy! I bless you! Now, go to your family and get them out! The schedule!"*

"What schedule?"

"Mrs. Appleyard's schedule. It has come due!"

His shouts were interrupted by a deep boom somewhere in the building. A high-pitched alarm sounded far away. Then another. I smelled smoke—for real this time.

"Her—*Mrs. Appleyard's* schedule? Is she—is she really?"

"Do you ever listen? She's burning down the building," said Alejandro. "Right now!"

I almost ran into Mrs. Appleyard when I stepped out of Alejandro's door. She stared at me, her eyes narrow. I heard someone call my name, over and over. It was Joanna. I pushed past Mrs. Appleyard and ran up the stairs.

I met Joanna on the second-floor landing. Her hands were shaking as she grabbed me. "I sold it," she said. "It's gone."

More smoke alarms joined in, shrieking at us. "We need to get out of here," I said. "The building is on fire."

Joanna said, "I know, but Alejandro—he practically begged me for it. For the bottle. I tried to talk him out of it, but he said he wanted it—and that it would bring no harm to him. Like he knew some way out. Anyway, it's gone, Gabe. It's gone. And we're—"

Joanna stopped mid-sentence when she noticed the bottle in my hand. She said, "Why do you have it?" She slumped down on the floor. "You—you bought it?"

I nodded.

"Why?"

"To save you," I said. "Can we talk about this later? The building is on fire!"

Joanna's mom was already hustling down the hallway with an armful of photo albums. I ran into my apartment.

All the smoke alarms were singing in unison now, like a choir from hell. Dad ran in after me, "Oh, thank God, Gabe. We just got home and couldn't find you outside. We have to get out of here. The building is on fire!"

Mom rushed in behind Dad. A few seconds later, she jammed a stack of photo albums into my arms—more than I could carry. "Take these and get outside."

"Photo albums? What is it with moms and photo albums?"

"Because everything else is replaceable. Now go!"

In the chaos, I set the bottle down on a table so I could hold the albums. We all ran out. Doctor Mandrake was in front of us on the stairs, shuffling his way down one step at a time.

"Hurry!" I shouted.

"I am doing my best," he said. "Oh! Sea Goat! My books! My crystals! My glow-in-the-dark stars! All shall be lost in the flames!"

We all tumbled out onto the front sidewalk. The building was belching smoke now. Shaky orange light showed through the black smoke. But at least we were all outside, all safe.

Mom stacked her photo albums on the sidewalk, next to piles of Jimmy Hyde's paintings wrapped in Hashimoto's red cloth. Dad was ticking off our names, making sure everyone was accounted for. "Alejandro, Joanna, Mrs. Sedley, Mandrake, Hashimoto, Hyde, all of us Silvers are here, right? One, two, three, four, and me—hey, where's Mrs. Appleyard?"

We all looked around. She was nowhere to be seen. Dad said, "Should one of us go back inside? Go look for her? Is she here?" Mom ran across the street to check at Hank's Bar. Dad stepped toward the building. Alejandro grabbed his arm. "It is not safe," Alejandro said. "And the firefighters should be here soon. We should wait for them."

"Wait? We can't wait! She could be dead by the time they get here."

"We should wait. Trust me."

Then I remembered the bottle. It was still inside. I knew it couldn't break, but what if it could burn? I was the owner now. If the bottle was destroyed, what would happen to my soul? Would I be free? Or damned?

"The bottle is still in there," I said to Joanna.

"What are you thinking?" said Joanna. "Don't go back inside. You can't."

"I've got to. Who knows what will happen if I don't." Before she could say another word, I ran—right through the front door, back into the fire. I heard voices shouting after me, begging me to stop.

I sucked in my breath and held it as I pounded up the stairs. I crashed into our apartment. I had to crouch low, as the smoke was thick near the ceiling. The air was hot. The fire must be nearby. It might burst through a wall or a floor at any second.

I squinted through the smoke and saw the bottle on the table, right where I left it. I grabbed it and the hot surface nearly burned my hand.

My lungs were straining for more air. I ran back through the door and made it halfway down the stairs before the air was clear enough for me to take a breath. I sucked in, then saw Mrs. Appleyard.

She stood on the stairway, blocking my path. Her hands gripped the railings on each side. "I want it, Ten Cents."

"Out of my way," I cried. "I can't die in here! I can't."

"I ain't letting you by unless you give it to me. That bottle. Right there."

A few feet above me, fire ate through the walls. "We need to get out of here! And I can't give it to you. I'd have to sell it to you."

"Then tell me a price."

"No! Let me by!"

"I seen you with it, Ten Cents, plenty of times. Heard you whispering about it. Seen Doctor Mandrake fussing over it. Took me a while, but I finally figured it. I know that's how you got all that stuff—that car, that hot tub. I know that's how the Brackleys got all-of-a-sudden rich again. Maybe that's how come Mrs. Sedley's all miracle-cured, too. A few too many miracles around here. So hand it over."

Smoke and heat forced me down another step until I was looking right in the face of Mrs. Appleyard.

"I told you, I can't just give it to you. I have to sell it."

"Name your price!" she shouted. I could just hear her above the screech of the smoke alarms and the roar of the fire.

"It's only a penny."

"A penny? Come on, Silver. The real price!"

"It really is a penny, but there's a cost to wishing on it! Your gain is someone else's loss. And your soul—the rules say that the next person who buys it will—well, the Devil will take them!"

"Ha! I don't care nothing about that! You've seen how I live. You know me. The truth of me. I reckon I'm going to the Devil anyway. And this bottle sounds like it could be the best thing I've struck yet."

A chunk of burning ceiling fell down between us. Mrs. Appleyard kicked it to the side. The stairway above me collapsed to the floor below. She reached inside her dress pocket and pulled out a penny. "If you're selling, I'm buying. Hand it over."

I coughed in the smoke. "I can't do that—not even to you."

"I'm giving you options, Ten Cents. Sell it to me, or the two of us are gonna die in here. And the Devil will take us both."

I gave in. I held out the bottle and took the penny in exchange. "Then I sell it to you, Mrs. Appleyard."

She wrapped her hands around the bottle. "It's mine now. And I'm selfish with my wishes, so you better scat."

She stepped aside. I rushed past her, took the rest of the stairs in two jumps, and ran out the door. I dove across the porch and landed on the sidewalk in a heap.

Just a few seconds later, the top two floors of the Bright House crashed to the ground. Fire roared out through the front door as if it was chasing me.

Joanna helped me to my feet. "Mrs. Appleyard—" I whispered.

We looked back at the building—the inferno. No one could go in there now. And no one was coming out. The smoke alarms had fallen silent, replaced by the roar of the fire and the sounds of fire trucks.

"Gabe," said Joanna, "the bottle. Where is it?"

"It's gone," I said. "Sold and gone."

"It's gone?" She rested her head on my shoulder. "Is it really gone?"

"It's gone," I said.

AND LAST

Dear Reader,

If you walk onto my block—well, my old block—you won't see the Bright House there anymore. Not a sooty beam. Not an ash.

It's all been cleaned up, but on a foggy day you can still smell the smoke. Of course, it could just be the smoke from all those years of Mrs. Appleyard's cigarettes.

In the spot where the Bright House used to stand is a shiny new home, with just one family living on the lot where all of us used to live: Doctor Mandrake, Mrs. Sedley, Joanna, Mom, Dad, Meg, Georgina, me, Lancaster, Mr. Brackley, Mrs. Brackley, Hashimoto, Jimmy Hyde, Alejandro Aguilar, and Mrs. Appleyard.

Dear Reader, count yourself lucky if you've never seen a building burn. It's terrifying and you'll never be able to forget it. The fire ate the Bright House like a twitchy orange monster, taking huge bites and burping out black smoke.

While we watched the firefighters try to control the

flames, Alejandro handed my dad a fat envelope. "Insurance information," he said. "You will need this in the morning." Then Alejandro drove away in a shiny pickup truck I'd never seen before. We never saw him again.

Jimmy Hyde and Hashimoto left in her red Lincoln Town Car. The rest of us—my family, the Sedleys, and Doctor Mandrake—caravanned to a nearby hotel. We ended up in adjoining rooms and went to bed.

In the morning, Dad called a phone number he found in the envelope. An insurance man met us all in the hotel lobby. He said the insurance would pay for us to stay at the hotel for thirty days. Then he handed out three checks: one to Doctor Mandrake, one to Mrs. Sedley, and one to Dad.

"Fifty thousand dollars each," explained Dad. "For what we lost in the fire."

"That seems like a lot of money for our junky old stuff," I said.

"Shhh," said Dad.

By the end of the month, Dad and Mom found a house— six blocks from Henry's house. It had regular-sized bedrooms and no holes in the living room ceiling. Dad used the insurance check and the leftover Ferrari money for a down payment.

Joanna and her mom moved into a downtown condo— farther away from me than I like, but Joanna and I still see each other at school every day. The first time we visited their condo, Henry said, "I like it, Mrs. Sedley. It's nice. But you know what it needs? More scarves. It's not scarfy enough."

Joanna punched Henry, right in the shoulder.

Mrs. Sedley is still healthy. In fact, Joanna said that she hasn't so much as caught a cold since the wish. Makes me wonder if she'll ever be sick again. She's back at work. Turns out she owns a vintage-clothing store. And in case you're wondering, Joanna still dresses all in black. Her mom even helps her find her dresses.

Dear Reader, some things don't change.

Doctor Mandrake used his money to lease a storefront on Sixth Avenue. In the store he sells dusty antiques, crystals, and rings with dragons on them—the same kooky stuff he had in his old top-floor apartment. He lives above the store and does his readings up there. By the way, Dear Reader, every specific prediction Mandrake made about Joanna came true. Every one. Go back and figure it out for yourself, if you don't believe me.

Sometimes Henry, Joanna, and I stop by Mandrake's to see what he has for sale. The last time we went in there— just one week ago—he said, "I have a prediction for you, young Sea Goat. For the rest of this year, your life will be boring, boring, boring."

"That doesn't sound very exciting," said Joanna.

"It's not," said Mandrake. "So you had better do something about it."

EPILOGUE

I thought that was the end of the story. I thought the bottle was gone from this world. And I never thought I'd hear from Mrs. Appleyard again, because I figured she had died. She was *the late* Mrs. Appleyard. She'd burned up in the fire and lost her soul to the Devil.

But then, just today, when Joanna was visiting, a photo postcard came in the mail. It showed a fishing boat, floating on an impossibly blue ocean.

On the back of the postcard was written:

Hey, Ten Cents. Greetings from El Pescadero. Turns out Mr. A was right. This fishing stuff is pretty fun after all.

"Who's it from?" asked Joanna.

"It's unsigned," I said. "But it's gotta be from Mrs. Appleyard." I handed it to Joanna. "She doesn't say much. But she doesn't seem too worried about her soul."

Joanna studied the picture, then laughed. "I don't think Mrs. Appleyard has ever worried about anything." She pointed to the name of the boat, painted along the bow in neat blue letters.

The name read: *THE WISH TO LIVE FOREVER.*

I laughed with Joanna. And you should laugh, too, Dear Reader.

Because even the Devil is no match for Mrs. Appleyard.

ACKNOWLEDGMENTS

I hand my first measure of thanks to Robert Louis Stevenson, for his dark, delicious words and for his short story "The Bottle Imp." Bob, I shamelessly used that story as my outline, and stole character names from so many of your tales to use as the names of my own heroes, villains, and supporting cast members. Another portion of thanks goes as ever to my agent and friend, the esteemed Abigail Samoun, for continuing to believe, to bolster, to cajole, and to remind me to include those damn Oxford commas. I present a well-crafted ration of thanks to my beloved city, Tacoma, for serving as the setting for another story. Thanks especially to K Street, where this story is fictionally set. That said, Tacoma mapmakers, we all know this street should rightfully be called MLK. You left out two key letters on your signs. I pass a large measure of thanks to Kelly Loughman, my brilliant editor at Holiday House, for her keen eye, her encouraging words, and her shared appreciation of Liz Lemon. Finally, all the gratitude that is left, as always, I hand to Deb. Thanks, hon. I owe you a back scratch.